Buffalo
Stew
For
Indigenous
Hearts

*To Kathleen,
I share this with
you out of friendship,
asking nothing in return.
Dan*

Dan E. Barden

1

Hawkesong Press
40 W. Littleton Blvd. 210-129
Littleton, Colorado 80120

(c)2001 Dan Barden

ISBN 0-9701542-1-6
Printed and Bound in the United States

Other Books by Dan Barden

"Andawehi, Sister of the Wolf"

Dedicated
to the
Great Spirit
Who Dwells Within
Us All.

"Great Spirit, once more behold me on earth and lean to hear my feeble voice. You lived first, you are older than all need, older than all prayer. All things belong to you, the two legged, the four legged, the birds of the air, and all green things that live."
"You have set the powers of the four quarters of the earth to cross each other. You have made me cross the good road, and the road of difficulties, and where they cross, the place is holy. Day in, day out, forevermore, you are the life of things."

Black Elk

Index

4

Welcome to Buffalo Stew

As a young boy, and still, as a man, my spirit
has been touched deeply by the wisdom of
the American Indian People.
They know the Great Spirit, and their place
in His Love.
They know the land, and the stewardship
that living on earth entails.
They know the animal and plant life, and
share a brotherhood with them as equals
in the Great Nations of all of
Earth's living things.
It is my wish here to share with you some
words from the true American Indian
Elders, as well as some short stories I have
written which, to me at least, apply
some of their reasoning and approach to
life
in different situations.

Thank You for reading,

Dan E. Barden

The Medicine of a Tree

As Indian people, we stand as a tree among rocks, bending and twisting with the fates of time, but being held in place by our roots. The tree's roots overcame the hardness of the rocks to find the water and nourishment they needed for the whole tree to live. Our roots have sustained us as well. That tree, like you and I both, owes everything in its existence to its roots. Should the tree, or any part of it become separated from its roots it would surely perish. The same is true of the People. Roots kept the tree upright, when the forces of nature could have caused it to fall. The same is true of the People. Roots kept the tree from trying to be something it was not. The same is true for the People. Roots gave the tree its identity, its sense of belonging to the Creator's perfect plan.

The same is true of the People. The settlers cut down many trees. They found that to be the easy part of clearing the land. But removing the roots of those trees was extremely difficult, a job that they did not expect. The same is true for the People, for many of our People were cut down, that was the easy part. But, unlike the tree, it was discovered that the roots of the People can never be erased from this land. Some have surely tried, with their alcohol, and drugs, and many of the People have fallen prey to their vices. And we pray for those fallen ones every day. But as long as there are those like you and me, who keep our roots nurtured and watered, they will continue to split the rocks, to find nourishment and sustenance. The voices of our ancestors, the Spirit of our People will never die nor leave the face of our Earth Mother. Without our roots, we are dead logs laying on the ground waiting to become mere kindling for the amusement of those who see little value in our existence."

The Sparrow and the Bear

There once lived a sparrow, who was born into more joy within himself than he saw in the world around him. He was born into a family of true, died in the wool sparrows, who could not see beyond their sparrowhood. He seemed to be always out of step with those he loved, and who were good to him. He could not understand why things he found joy and meaning in, they saw as frivolous and meaningless. He knew early on that if he were to face this life and be true to himself, it was going to be a challenge, for what he was being taught, was not what he wanted to learn.

He had always heard the call of the wild geese flying overhead, the songs of the mountains, and the voices of the other animals, that his family and friends seemed to be blinded and deafened to. The natural world spoke to him in great harmony, and he found his heart was in the simple things, the priceless free gifts the Creator gives to all with love. He tried to live as those around him did, for many, many years. All that their ways brought him was more emptiness of Soul, and a greater appreciation of the voices of Spirit speaking through all living things.   The clothing he wore was not the clothing of his Spirit, and he knew this.

So it was not a surprise when the fates of life, after many years of trying left him broke, but not defeated. And in that Soul searching and Soul facing event, he knew that it was time for him to live as his heart called him, to answer the gentle voice within. So he left his home of many years, and a family that loved him, and, other than his son, a family that did not understand him.

He answered the call of the mountains. One of the happiest days of his life was when he pointed himself west, with a new sense of freedom and being, and flew to the mountains.

He took in all of the beauty there, the flora and fauna, the majesties that always point to the heavens and reminded him of the Source of all love and life.   The simplicity which he sought was all around him now, in the beauty that is offered to all who will see. He was still in the Sparrow world, to be sure, but there was more open space here, more things in nature to stimulate and nurture his Spirit, and he chose to participate in the daily mundane things as little as necessary. In his free time, he flew through the back country, in the valleys and over the mountain tops, dancing on the wind with feelings of peace and joy that had long been sought by his Spirit, but rarely experienced. He would often land in an evergreen beside a mountain stream, and let the waters sing to his Soul, as if mesmerized. This was the true thing, he thought, where my Spirit has sought to fly, as myself, without the "shoulds" of my fellow sparrows. He bathed in the cool mountain lakes and streams. If a day was uncomfortably warm, he flew to the peaks, and played in the snow still there from winters past. The gifts of Spirit that he found in the mountains renewed in him his Life Force, and took his mind away from the past, and more into the "Now."

After about a year of living there, and enjoying the freedom of Spirit and Being that was now his, he again began to sense a stirring in his Spirit. He came to realize that the problem was in himself, and that the beauty of the mountains was only to set the stage for him to seek freedom and growth, unfettered by the past. The stirring within his heart was loneliness, for though he was living in a place of his dreams, he began to see that it is not the place that makes us happy, it is the living in sync with our Heart and Spirit.

His loneliness was beginning to challenge his serenity, and he knew he could not give in to this negative energy that was pursuing him. He spent many days, even months, flying to places of great beauty and warmth, trying to get his heart in a place where it could receive the answers he needed, away from his Sparrow feelings.

He was flying over new, uncharted territory one day, when he spotted a clear mountain lake more beautiful than he had ever seen. The water was as pure a turquoise as it could be. Majestic evergreens stood around its shores, as if waiting to get their chance to jump in. Red Rock outcroppings provided the balcony to this wonderful Cathedral created by God. He had never found the Love and Joy of the Great Spirit anywhere more than here.

He flew around in circles over this beautiful place, as if awestruck by the light emanating from a priceless gem. Something about this place called to him, and he slowly flew down to the shores of this glowing lake, to rest on its shores. He had no fears here, he was in total beauty, and nothing that could harm him was around.

He heard a rustling behind him, and turned around to see a beautiful female bear coming towards him. While she did not strike fear in him, he was wary.

"Good afternoon, My Son," she spoke softly, "I have been expecting you"

"You will not harm me will you, Lady Bear?" he asked.

"Of course not, My Son, I am here to help you, to offer you help you have long sought, but never found."

"But how did you now I was coming?"

"There are many who know all about you, who know all about everyone,
The Great Spirit grants to the seekers of worthiness, so that they may help others."

"I want to find out who I am, for I have never found comfort living within the limitations of a sparrow, never have. And unless I am my true self, I will always be lonely and out of step, I am afraid"

"You can know this, I will help you, but not without risks of losing yourself in the process."

"How do you mean? I fear I have already lost myself, or at least never been myself."

"You must have strong faith, for this is not a game to be played."

"Lady Bear, help me.............nothing I have ever done has brought me the inner peace I seek on a consistent level, for even now, the beauty of this place is not enough, I know there is more, and I want to take my Spirit to where there is more."

"My son, it is an all or nothing deal, as your life on earth goes, you will risk all that you are, to hopefully become all that you think you are."

"If what you are, is all you are, then you will pass from this earth before your time. But if there is more to you, as you believe, you will be born anew in that which you truly are, to live as you have never known life before. How strongly do you believe in your quest, My Son?"

"But I don't understand, tell me more, please."

"My Son, what you are now is what you have done with the gifts that the Great Spirit bestowed up on you in your creation. You are the sum of all your actions. Perhaps, unknowingly to you, you have not used your strengths as much as you have your weaknesses. You have not allowed yourself to dance to the music that the Creator Spirit placed within your soul. And if that is the case, your faith will give you a new way of living, or if your faith is false, and only based on wishes, it shall pass you back to Spirit immediately."

"How do I do this, for my faith is strong? I would rather be back in the world of Spirit than living as out of sync as I am"

"See that high red cliff off to the Northwest?"

"Yes, there seem to be others there"

"Yes there are others there..............we are now in a place of Magic.........few know of this place, for many, their hearts do not call them to seek which they do not see, or what they can only feel........their quest is only in that which can be authenticated by the senses of their physical bodies..............You, me, and others here, however, seek what our Spirits reveals to us, and our Souls overhear, and our hearts undertake..............it is not this lake that is magical........as much as it is you and I, and everyone who chooses magic are magical.........we come here to begin to live that magic within us, to be born anew into all its wonders.........think yourself to that high cliff, and I will meet you there.......just see yourself there, and you are there."

In an instant there they were, on a high cliff of red rock, where they could see mountain peaks for ever, pointing to the Great Spirit above. Cotton puff clouds passed silently overhead, as if they were the footprints of Angels in heaven. Far below, the beautiful turquoise water of the lake, in its crystal clarity glowed as bright as the sunshine bathing them all.

"Now what," he asked, as he took in the beauty around him.

"Observe, and listen"

As they watched, a Raven stood on the edge of the high cliff. He seemed to be preparing himself to jump off it. Sparrow looked at the Lady Bear, as if to say "Stop Him!" Lady Bear just shook her head, and with her piercing eyes, commanded the Sparrow to silence and observation.

The Raven held his wings tight to his sides, and shouted out the word "NOW" and descended head first to the lake far below. Sparrow watched in amazement, and bewilderment.

Just before Raven was to hit the water, he pulled back, in a lack of faith, opened his wings, and flew level with the lake...........but he did not fly long, for a hawk descended on him and took him back to feed her young.

Next up, a frog stood on the edge, with his head down, getting ready to spring into the unknown on his faith alone.

"Now" he shouted, and as he fell towards the water, he could be heard screaming happily............"I am free, I am free." And he hit the water, there was silence. Then a rumbling of the water, and out stepped a beautiful Majestic Bull Elk.

The elk looked up towards the High Cliff, nodded its head in respect, bowed, and gave thanks for a moment, and walked into the woods to explore the life it had dreamed of.

Next up, a rabbit, who stood on the edge, shaking in fear. "NOW" the rabbit said, and jumped off into the turquoise waters. Rabbit hit the waters, and remained a rabbit, lifelessly laying on the surface of the beautiful lake. Another hawk swooped in, carried the rabbit away to feed her young.

"Do you get the picture, My Son," asked the Lady Bear?

"Kinda," replied Sparrow, please help me.

"Raven failed because of his lack of faith, and his lack of true knowledge about who he was. He could not risk it all, as the thought he could. But like I told you, the risk is taken when leaving the rock, there is no turning back."

"Frog had strong faith, and a great knowledge of himself, and what he was. His knowledge and faith was answered when he hit the water, and emerged as the bull elk. He knew he was more than what he had become, and risked it all, because his faith was strong."

"Rabbit had the faith, but he was already all he could be. He misjudged his calling, and never learned to be happy with who he was. His faith was more based in false illusions of grandeur in himself, than in his heart calling him to fulfill his purpose."

"So now you know how this works, what true faith can take you to, what false faith will bring you. How happy are you REALLY with who you

17

are, and how strong and sincere is your faith?"

"Lady Bear, I cannot go on as I am, and I know there is more to me than I have let myself know, and if this is my end, then so be it, but I cannot go on as I am."

"Sparrow, my son.............you are wise enough to know that you cannot lose. Raven is out of his misery as is Rabbit, back to the Spirit world where they do not ache, or hurt, or torture themselves with thoughts about what might have been. There are no losers here, for Spirit is timeless and ever evolving, each in our own way, each in our own time. You have come here to be released, and be released you will. But remember one thing, my little friend.........once you step to the edge of that rock and jump, you will never be the same............never again will you walk in the body you step up there with, or know that which you possess now..............This is not a gamble, any more than crossing any bridge is, or taking any passage. After your jump, you will never be the same, and is this not what you wish the most?"

"Lady Bear, though I have known you only for a few moments, it is as if we have walked for a lifetime. Something tells me we will walk more."

"Just in case you wondered, My Son, before I jumped, I was a serpent."

"NOW", sparrow said in a voice as loud as he

could muster, with wings tucked tightly to his sides. He hit the water full bore, and after a few moments of calm, out of the water arose a beautiful Bald Eagle, flying proudly.

"What is life? It is the flash of a firefly in the night.
.......the breath of the buffalo in the winter time
.......a little shadow which runs across the grass,
and loses itself in the sunset. "

Crowfoot

A Wing and a Prayer

He settled back in his window seat on the big jetliner. The plane had just left Detroit Metro Airport to take Dr. Ben Movingwater back to his home, and his people in Tulsa. He had spent ten years in the state of Michigan, attending University of Michigan Medical School in Ann Arbor, and serving his two year residency at a Hospital in Sault Ste. Marie, where he could serve and help his fellow Indian People. He was Cherokee, and Michigan is the land of the Anishinabe, the People of the Three Fires, the Ojibwa, the Ottawa, and the Potawatomie. Ben had many friends he was leaving behind, and a greater love and understanding for all people from his time in College, Medical School, and Residency.

He looked out the window at a setting sun, and

thought of how long he had waited for this day. He was of the Wolf Clan, and the Great Spirit often came to him as the Wolf, his guide and Spirit animal. As he relaxed his mind, and focused on his Spiritual side, the Wolf appeared outside his window. He was called to prayer. Silently he spoke,

"Great Spirit, a day I have dreamed of is here, and I give thanks to You for allowing me this journey and path. I give thanks for the opportunity to return to my home and family, and contribute what You have allowed me to learn for the good of all. I am humbled by Your power, for I know that as my hands treat and heal it will be Your love and strength working through them and doing the healing. I pray that my hands will always be worthy to be tools of Your love and healing power. I pray that my ears will always be open to Your loving voice and guidance, and that my eyes will always see the path that You wish for me to take."

"You have set before me, people of all races who are sick and need your healing, and I thank You for this, for you remind me that as an Indian, I do not just wish to heal my people, but all people. As an Indian, I look for the day when all men walk together as one clan in Your love. I believe that day will come, maybe not in my

22

lifetime, for You have not handed down Your word that it would. Let me be a tool of Yours to help bring this day about. The Earth will be glorious, and all Glory to You now and when that day comes."

"Great Spirit, you have taught me to be true to my Spirit, not the color of my skin, and I give you thanks for this. I pray for all people, that they may receive Your blessings, and hear and feel your love in the beautiful world You have placed us in. I pray that when a patient comes before me, their race and skin color will be forever blinded from my eyes."

"Great Spirit, please keep me ever mindful of the ways I have been taught. Let the Ancient Truths live through me, and let me enjoy the closeness and kinship to nature that my People have always enjoyed. I pray that You keep me off the trail of materialism, and keep me ever mindful that the only possessions of any value are the possessions of Spirit and Heart, the things we can give away in this life, and take to the next one. Always keep me mindful that, if I have something here on earth, I do not own it, I am just its caretaker while I am here, and since I do not own it, it belongs to everyone."

"This is my prayer to you, Great Spirit."

*"Love is something you and I must have.
We
must have it because our Spirit feeds on it.
We must have it because without it we
become
weak and faint. Without love our self-
esteem
weakens. Without it our courage fails.
Without
love we can no longer look out at the world
confidently."*
*"Without love, we turn inward and begin to
feed
on our own personalities, and little by little
we destroy ourselves."*

Chief Dan George

Let me be your Brother

Let me be your brother,
Let me shake your hand,
Let me hear the words you speak,
Help me understand.

We can see we're different,
Our clothes, our speech, our skin,
But we both give off the Light of God,
That comes from deep within.

We both have known our sorrows,
We both have known our pain,
We've known our days of sun,
And slept out in the rain.

Heartbreak, it has found us both,
And strength came from up above.
We've heard our beloved ones' dying breath,
And sent them Home in Love.

We've held the little children close,
And taught them not to fear,
And told them everything's OK,
As long as Daddy's here.

Our Elders we have sat and heard,
The power in their ways,
And wish to keep their words alive,
Throughout our living days.

We both have built our homes with hands,
That ache when day is done,
And built them back again and again,
As storm clouds hid the sun.

So, though we may look different,
In our hearts we're both the same,
With dreams and hopes for one's we love,
And those who our love claim.

So I honor you, my brother,
And your ways that are not like mine.
And I wish to learn the Path you walk,
And look forward to the time,

When all men walk as brothers,
Not just the likes of me and you.
And through the clouds of circumstance,
The Great Spirit's Love comes shining through.

Only in America

Andawehi and her grandfather were traveling from Denver to Wolcott, Colorado for a couple days of camping. It was evening, it had been a long day. Grandfather was 101 years old, quite spry for his age, and he only spoke and understood the Cherokee language. He was about as traditional as anyone could be, with his long braided ponytail, and hat with an Eagle feather in it. Andawehi loved her grandfather more than anyone else on earth.

"Grandfather, it will not be long until we are at the place where the eagles dance. We have not eaten, shall we stop to get something? We can always eat in the car," Andawehi said in the Cherokee tongue they shared.

"Sounds like good idea," said Grandfather, hardly

paying any attention as he took in the grandeur of the high mountains in the light of the setting sun.

"Do you care where we stop?", asked Andawehi.

"No, not as long as we do not go to the place of clowns. Clown remind me of witches I was taught to fear as a child. No clowns."

To say the least, Grandfather was not a fan of McDonald's. He would go there if it meant making his great great grandchildren happy, but definitely not if there was any other way of getting something to eat.

Andawehi smiled and chuckled to herself, shaking her head, "Grandfather is so consistent, and true to his ways. Him and his fear of clowns."

As they pulled onto an exit ramp at the town of Silverthorn. Andawehi was feeling the need to stretch her legs, and breath some fresh air.

"Grandfather, shall we eat at Arby's at the sign of the big cowboy hat?", asked Andawehi.

"Sounds like good idea," said Grandfather, still staring up at the beautiful mountains.

As they walked inside, the sight of the young girl behind the counter captured the attention of Grandfather. He stopped and stared at her, as if she was a vision from his childhood. He then got on the other side of Andawehi, away from the girl, as if Andawehi would protect him.

"What, they got clowns here too now?" asked grandfather seriously, "orange hair, all that metal holding her face together, what is going on?"

The young woman heard Grandfather speak in Cherokee and she asked Andawehi what he was saying. This kind of caught her off guard, so she replied,

"This is my grandfather, he only speaks Cherokee language. He was just telling me that he loves the freedom that you young people have to dress as you wish."

"Tell him Thank You for me, not many old folks like this get up," the girl replied.

Grandfather kept insisting, "Is that woman talking about me, I ask you?"

In Cherokee, Andawehi replied, "Eduda, she

is just a girl who works here.   That is the way some of the young people   choose to dress today."

"You mean she looks like that on purpose?" asked Grandfather as he smacked his hands together and shook his head.

Andawehi chuckled.   The girl asked what grandfather said.   Andawehi told her that Grandfather admired her individuality.

With that, she asked Grandfather to go sit down, and she would bring him his food. She did not know how much of this she could take.

"Tell your grandfather that I wish I had long braided hair like he has, please?" the girl asked of Andawehi.

"What did she say about me?", Grandfather asked quickly.

"Eduda, that girl says she wishes that she had long braided hair as pretty as yours."

"Horse dribble," replied Grandfather.

"What did he say," asked the girl?

"He said sounds like good idea," replied Andawehi.

"He doesn't smile much for a guy saying such nice things, does he?" asked the young girl.

Grandfather again quickly asked Andawehi what the girl was saying about him?

"She says you look hungry, Eduda."

"Not hungry as I was," replied Grandfather.

"And no, miss, he does not smile much when he is in awe of what he sees."

Andawehi could take no more, after many stern looks, she gritted her teeth and told grandfather to go sit down, and directed his arm toward the seating area she wanted.

"Sounds like good idea," he mumbled under his breath.

As they left the Arby's, Grandfather turned around to get one last look at the young woman. She waved, smiled, and blew kiss at him. He wrinkled up his face as if sucking on a raw lemon, and said "Horse dribble", as he went out the door.

"Whenever in the course of the daily hunt, the hunter comes across a scene that is strikingly beautiful--a black thundercloud causing the rainbow to arch over the mountains, a white waterfall in the heart of a lush green gorge, a vast prairie tinged with the blood red of the sunset, he pauses for an instant in the attitude of worship."
"He sees no need for setting apart one day in seven as holy, for to him, all days are holy."

Ohiyesa

Loneliness

"How can people ever feel alone in the wilderness, with our brother's and sisters of the animal nations around us?"

"My dear Andawehi, the elders taught that great loneliness of Spirit comes to those who do not recognize the gifts that the animals bring. Many people today suffer from this great loneliness of Spirit because their eyes can see no farther than the credit card in their hand. Their ears hear no more than the sounds of machinery, their fine cars, and their music makers. Their noses cannot smell beyond the smoke from their life altering cigarettes, or the smog from those cars. Their tastes know nothing more than the chemicals in their manufactured foods. Their feet do not know the wonderful sensations of walking barefoot on our earth mother. Few know the joy of hearing the Eagle sing or the solace one can find in the gentleness of a mother deer nursing its young. The Creator speaks to us everywhere, through the gifts He gives us in nature. You are so right, I share your wonder how a man can be lonely with the rich medicine of the animals and nature all around us."

"Our people knew thousands of years ago what people are trying to get back now. That inner peace that comes from being in balance with everything around you. We do not kill an animal without asking permission of its Spirit to do so. We do not scar the countryside to make baubles for our own adornment. This great emptiness of Spirit that has overtaken society today is caused from a turning away from the ancient truths, and hearts being closed to the message of the Creator who speaks through his plants and animals. Hearts have become focused on the works of man, and closed to the works of the Great Spirit. Today man tries to fill the empty spaces with things that only touch the pleasure centers. And yet man walks and dwells in a world where the loving voice of the Great Spirit is always singing beautiful songs. If we can let ourselves be awed by nature's beauty and music, we will receive great lessons in Spirituality which will keep us in balance."

7

Old Ways, Young People

This was a special night for Elder Ben Greenleaf, eldest living member of his tribe. Some of the young people of the tribe had come to him and asked him if he would tell them about the old ways, the ancient traditions. He was honored to do so. He asked them to prepare a fire at the east end of the lake near the village. He would meet them there after the setting sun gave light to the first star to be seen. He told them that if they wanted to hear of the old ways, it would be done in the old ways. They were to circle the campfire, in silence, and he would bring his talking stick with him, and ONLY the one with the talking stick would get to speak.

He chose the east end of the lake, for it was about a half hour walk from the village. He wanted to make sure the young people had time to experience the quietness of the evening returning as a friend. He wanted the song of the loon, and the yip of the coyote to dull their awareness of their fast paced lives, and let the sounds and songs of nature sing some preparatory hymns for their Spirits. He also wanted their cars to be not at hand, with their accompanying music and distractions, nor fun loving friends stopping in to disturb the moment.

As he approached the fire surrounded by the young ones, Ben was pleased that silence drowned out all but the songs of the insects. He was also pleased that 7 young people had come to this place. He felt good about the Spirit of the evening.

Ben sat down in the open space left for him. He took the hands of those on both sides of him, and nodded for all to follow, which they did. He raised his arms, and his head toward the sky,

"Great Spirit, who lives within us all,
Thank you for bringing us together in your honor.
If some hearts here are closed, let your message open them,

If some are sad, let your inspiration let them know joy,
And always, let your Great Love flow to, and through us, your children."

As everyone put their hands down, one young man, named Puma stood up and turned his back to walk away. Ben threw the talking stick in front of him, landing in his path. Puma turned around, and Ben made a motion for him to pick up the stick and talk. Puma bent over, with his long black hair touching the ground, grabbed the stick, and walked back to the circle.

"I did not know this was going to be a revival service, I thought you were going to teach us of the old ways." Puma tossed the stick back to Ben.

Ben said, "My friends, the Spirituality of our people, as a Nation, was first and foremost to our ancestors. It was secondary to nothing in their lives. It was the foundation on which a successful life was built on, it was life itself. If speaking about, and to, the Great Spirit offends you, you have nothing to learn about your ancestors, and you may continue on your way, my son."

Puma put his head down, as if embarrassed, and

again took his seat in the circle.

"In the ancient ways of our people, meaning before the arrival of the Europeans, our ancestors did not know "good" or "evil", or "Heaven" or "Hell". Everything, even death was met with acceptance, as the will of the Creator. Judgment was not passed on every event or person. There were many unpleasant things for our ancestors, and there always will be for people living on this earth. But because something was unpleasant, it was not labeled as "bad". Judgment and labels were two words our ancestors would not relate to.
They did not waste time analyzing, ruing, sulking; for their efforts were concentrated on rising above unpleasantness, pain, and sorrow. They worked hard, individually and as a Nation, to make themselves Spiritually strong so life did not overwhelm them."

Feather, a young lady in the group looked like she was going to explode, wanting to speak, so Ben tossed her the talking stick.

"Ben, with all due respect, how can you say the People did not recognize good or evil? Everything is either good or evil, that is the way it is. Did our ancestors live with their head in the sand?" She tossed the stick back to Ben.

"Remember, I am speaking of pre-European arrival times. I am telling you of the way our ancestors lived. There was One Creator. There was One Spirituality. The was One nation of like people, and one Creator. It was the European people, through their religion that taught our ancestors good and evil, heaven and hell. And while one is living in fear of hell and evil, he cannot focus his mind on the wonder of his Maker. To the Ancient Aboriginal People, this was not even a consideration."

Ben tossed the stick to a young man called Crow.

"Ben," he said, "you are talking out of both sides of your mouth. You are calling the European belief's bad, and saying the Indian ways are good." He tossed the stick back to Ben.

"Crow, you have just proven my point. You have been captured by the Society that invented good versus bad. I have not spoken badly of the European faith, I have pointed out a big difference between it and the Ancient Indian faith. It is you, who has been taught this Good-Bad thing, you just used it on me. Any Faith system which opens a man's heart to the Creator's Love is relevant and to be honored.

Try to rid yourself of this Good-Bad way of thinking. I have yet to say anything is bad, have I?" He tossed the stick back to Crow.

"No, you haven't. I misunderstood you." Crow tossed the talking stick to a young woman called Dove.

"Ben, I am mystified by your words about evil not existing. Please explain." She threw the stick back to Ben.

"OK, as an example, what is darkness?" Ben asked. "Is it a proactive force you can create? Think about this."
"Can you flip a switch and turn on darkness? Or is darkness a reactive force that exists only in the absence of light?" Many moments of silence passed.
"With light present, darkness cannot exist, can it?"
"Is it not true that the only way you can create darkness is remove light?" Many more moments of silence passed. Soon, everyone was nodding their heads in agreement with Ben's reasoning.

"Okay, now let's move a step further to the ancestor's way of thinking. Love is Light. For our purposes here, the thing called Evil is darkness. Everyone with me?"

40

Nodding heads greeted him, some smiling, as if catching on.

"Is Love a proactive force? Think about this. I think you will agree that Love is the most powerful force in the universe. We can turn it on, nothing can stop the Creator's love which flows through us."

The circle nodded in agreement.

"Okay, what is this thing called Evil? Can it exist in the presence of Love? NO!!! Evil can only exist in the absence of Love, just as Darkness can only exist in the absence of Light. Why do you think Evil and Darkness are so often associated, yet darkness was never an unpleasant word to the Indian? Darkness is the balance of the day. Darkness allows us to see the stars and the universe."

"Now, can you see why the Spiritual well being of all the people of the Nations was so important, from the least to the Greatest? Because if the Creator's Love filled the hearts of all people, Evil could never be given space to be."

"In my opinion, it was largely owing to their deep contemplation in the silent retreats in the days of youth that the Indian orators acquired the habit of carefully arranging their thoughts."
"They listened to the warbling of birds, and noted the grandeur and the beauties of the forest. The majestic clouds, the golden tints of a summer evening sky, and all the changes of nature possessed a mysterious significance.
"All of this combined to furnish ample matter for reflection to the youth in contemplation."

Ohiyesa

Mother and Child

Andawehi recalled the time when she was about eight years old, that her mother came out to the barn and sat down to talk with her. She was worried that Andawehi was working too hard on the farm, and not taking time for fun. The shine in Andawehi's eyes was dimming, her mother and father both noticed. They appreciated her hard work and dedication to the family operation, but wanted to see her have fun and take time to be a child. She adored both her parents greatly, and always went out of her way to contribute to the workings of the ranch, and honor her parents in this way.

Her mother called her aside after she had cleaned the stalls in the stud barn. Mom asked her to quit for the evening, and take time for herself.

"But mother," replied Andawehi, "Bobbie is sick, and if I do not clean the stalls of the foals, they will not get done today. And I do not want to see Father have to do them after he gets home from work."

She worried about her father, who drove truck many hours a day, and then came home and worked on the farm, where his heart was the happiest.

"My Darling Andawehi," her mother said softly, "the work will get done. You are working too hard. You are not taking time for yourself, for the things you enjoy, and the moments that make your Spirit dance. You know how proud your father and I are of you, and how honored we are by the work you do here, but we want to see you laugh and have fun too. We are concerned about you."

"Oh Mother, you are such a mother, and as such, you worry too much about me. It is my joy to be of help to you and father, and you know how much I love the horses. Besides, when our family goes to the Pow Wow, and I can dance in front of you , dad, and Grandfather, that is fun to me."

"But my daughter, you too are a mother, and

you are neglecting your child," mom said.

"Silly Mom, I am not a mother, why do you say this?" Andawehi asked.

"Yes, my daughter, you indeed are a mother, and in your care is the most wonderful child you will ever know."

Andawehi was puzzled, and she loved it when her mother spoke to her in this way as she often did, in a way that made her go within herself and think.

"You are the mother of the child within you, that Sacred part of you that is innocence and wonder. There must be more fun for you in your life than dancing in your regalia at the Pow Wows."

"I fear you are not taking care of nor nurturing your child. Work is good, never hurt anyone, it teaches us to be disciplined and to give of ourselves for the common good."

"As we nurture you, and allow you to grow into the strong individual that you are, you must nurture yourself. The child in you will always be present, and life as an adult will be cold and empty if you do not take your child with you."

"Life in this modern world will attempt to change you, make you cold and hard with its unforeseen problems and challenges. Your inner child will allow you to stay close to what is you, what your father and I have been trying to instill in you. You are Indian, and in this world you will know many hardships and twists of fate. But if you nurture this child that is you, none of these things will ever overcome your Spirit, and you will be able to laugh and give thanks for the Lady you are, and your abilities to rise above hardship."

Andawehi gave her mother a huge hug, and set the pitchfork in its place on the wall, and headed for the lake on their ranch, where she loved to play, and exercise her dreams, as well as her muscles.

The teachings of her mother, father, and grandfather were always close to her surface. They seemed to come out when needed, and she again realized what a fountain of wisdom she had to draw from in every situation in which she found herself.

9

Soul Pictures

She now focused her eyes on a baby picture of Tawodi's that was on the mantle of the fireplace. Beside it was a picture of her when she was just starting school. The pictures took her back to a time when they were together and Tawodi explained something to her that he felt strongly about, and after hearing it from him, so did she. Tawodi was a deep thinker, he had a way of looking at things that brought home ways of being to her that she had never thought of. This was one of the reasons she felt he was more red than white, because of the way he saw life, and all of its peculiarities, and the way he saw them always seemed to coincide with the red ways she was taught.

She fondly remembered him telling her,

"I have a theory, it is that when you look at a child or baby picture of an adult, you are looking at a picture as close as we can come to that person's Soul. Not their Soul per se, but how we perceive see their soul."

"The providence of joy and good humor belongs to the children. And since this is true, it can and should also belong to adults, the people children evolve into. Although it too often happens, the Spirit that is present in the child is not just automatically taken away when that child becomes an adult. And we, as adults, do not allow other adults to be a child. We "blind" ourselves to that Spirit of joy and good humor in ourselves, as adults, and do not always encourage its long life in children."

"I guarantee you, if you are ever mad at someone, and are having trouble seeing much good in them, take out a child picture of that person, and with little trouble, you will see the joy and goodness in them. You will see the hope and faith that they brought with them to this life. You will lose your perception of an adult that has hurt you in some way, and see the child in them that is as close to a Soul Picture as you can get. You will see that our Creator created each of us to be happy, to know and share love and joy in life. You will see that person free of all of the adjectives that make you look down on them now. Try it the next time you are upset with one of your children, or me. As you know, I have been upset with you many times, and every time I look at that picture of you, the frivolity of my feelings at that moment become apparent, and I again see you as the precious child of God that you are."

10

Red Guidance

Her name was Nellie Whitehawk. She had just graduated from Oklahoma University last spring, and was a couple of months into her new job as a counselor at her old Alma Mater, Sequoya High School in Talequah Oklahoma. It was a great honor for her to return here as an educator to the youth of her people, and her dream was to give back to the Nation that had guided her this far in life. She was raised in the Cherokee traditions, and earnestly believed in the importance and necessity of keeping them alive.

Nellie was working on some student profiles when a knock came to her door.

"Come in," she said.

It was a young man she knew as Colt, a freshman athlete, who was well thought of and known throughout the school.

"Hi, Ms. Whitehawk, do you have time to speak with me?"

"Yes, of course, Colt," she replied. She could tell by the redness of his eyes that he was troubled, and had been crying.

"Come in, and tell me what is bothering you."

Through teary eyes he spoke,

"You know I play football. Practice begins in about a half hour."

"Yes, Colt."

"I know this is wrong, but I hate the coach, I hate the assistant coach, and I hate the game of football and the people I play it with."

Nellie was taken back. This young man had it all. He was a star runningback as a freshman, he was looked up to by the upperclassmen, and respected by all who knew him.

"Colt, I do not understand, please tell me why you feel this way."

"My mom and dad. It will kill them if I do not play football like my two older brothers did, only it is not enough that I play, I must be better than them. I cannot take this, it is killing me."

"But we are two months into the season, why did it not come to you until now?"

"Ms Whitehawk, I have tried, I have really tried, and I always give my best, but I feel I am being true to what others want of me, and not myself."

"Please give me an example, Colt, of why you feel this way," Nellie said, as she passed a box of tissue to him.

"I am taking Speech class, just left there. Kids are practicing for debate and forensics programs to compete with other schools. That is where my heart is, in the expression of my Spirit, the social intercourse of issues we face. I watch those kids, and I wish I was one of them, but I can't be, for they practice when football does. I enjoy Speech class more than any other I take, even Phys. Ed."

"So you feel you are not "yourself", is that it?

"Yes, that is it, and I am only a freshman, if I continue to let others direct me, then my high school years will not be too happy."

"Colt, can I talk to you 'Skin to 'Skin?"

"Yes, of course, Ms. Whitehawk."

"You are 14 years old, you are at the age when few at that age know who they are. You have an inkling of who you are, but it is not yet clear, and that is OK, it will come if you seek it."

"When we do not know ourselves, and this is true of adults as well as children, we are like a spider. We weave a web, hoping to catch something or someone that we can see as meaningful. We latch on to things we catch in our web, and they often turn out to be much less than we first saw in them. We go external to ourselves and neglect the Voice within. We often hate and despise that which we caught. Are you following me?"

"Yes."

"When we hate, we keep that which we hate stuck in our web, where we remain connected to it, and it zaps energy from us. Your have woven a web in regards to playing football, and it is consuming you. Your parents are in this web, for you fear their disapproval should you let it go. Still with me?"

"Yes."

"When you learn who you are, and the songs that your heart sings, and you act out of this knowledge, and not the expectations of others, you will no longer weave webs, for you will have all you need. The approval of others will not matter, for you will become your own expression of the Spirit that is YOU! You are not there yet, but you can move in that direction, for you are aware of the difference."

"Then , football is NOT me. Right?"

"Colt, I cannot say that, for only you know. But I do feel you are not playing for the love of a game, you are playing for the love of your parents, and that is not true, they will love you no matter what. And," she hesitated, "you are not playing for Colt, you are playing against the Ghosts of your two older brothers. I see a big diffrence."

"Yes, I have to be myself, right?"

"Yes, but before you shoot off in 20 directions, you have to know that "Self" that is you. Spend time in quiet, thinking of these things. Become comfortable with who YOU are, not with what others think you should be."

"Once you become you, the real you, the

personification of the music within you, you will know what is right and wrong for you. You will work to keep the YOU manifested. You will recognize opportunities that will bring you success, and turn away from ones that will not. Life is full of choices, and you will make wiser ones. You will dream more, and you will see ways to bring those dreams alive and know them."

"A Hawk does not behave like a lizard. He knows he is a Hawk, and seeks perfection as one. If he misses out on a rabbit, he does not try and turn into a cow or a snake. If he misses a meal, he sharpens his skills, and hunts with a greater vengeance next time. Because he knows who and what he is, he lives without fear. He knows he will eat again."

"Many people fear who they are, for their comfort zone has always been in being directed by others. I do not feel this is the case with you, Colt."

"Thank You Ms. WhiteHawk. I am going to skip football practice today, and spend some time back in the woods."

"I am here for you, Colt, Donadagohvi"

54

11

Hands

"Look at these hands," said Grandfather. "They have held a beautiful woman, ten children, 28 grandchildren, 42 great grandchildren. They have been cut and scarred, and bruised and broken, but they still serve me well. The story of my life is the story of what these hands have held. They have held my children and grandchildren as they came into this world. And they have held some of them as they left. They have held my beautiful Morningstar as she crossed over, as well as both of my parents. These hands have known the celebration of new life, and the sadness of life passing."

"They have built homes for my loved one's to live in, and they have picked up the pieces of homes destroyed by powers much greater than I. They have never been used to hit another in vain, they have never held a gun aimed at another man, and they have never clapped at the misfortune of another."

"Each of us is the product of the hands that have touched us. A child who has been touched by hands that communicated love will know love and share love through his/her hands. One who has been touched mainly by hands that hurt will know anger and spite, and use its hands to perpetuate those feelings. Worse yet, probably, is the child that has not been touched by hands at all, or rarely. The world must be a very empty place to one such as that."

"It was always my wish that my hands gave out nothing but love and comfort to those who I touched. Creator above, I thank you for these hands, and I pray that their work was always pleasing to you, Great Spirit."

12

How the Mountains Came to Be

"There was a time when the earth had many moons. It was hard to tell the difference between the evening and the daylight. The Earth was flat. The brightness of all of the moons in the night sky made it look like daylight, and in the daytime the moons blocked out the sunlight.

I believe it was brother Owl who first complained of this. Brother Owl said that he was a creature of the night, that he had trouble seeing in the light of day, and needed the night to be able to open his eyes and hunt and provide for his family.

Then Brother Eagle spoke, and said that as the messenger of the Creator, he needed high places to meditate and contemplate, to be close to the Creator so he could hear the Creator's messages and deliver them to the Earth.

Then Brother Coyotee spoke up. He said he spoke for the furbearers, the Raccoon, the Wolf, the Beaver and all of the creatures who wore heavy fur. He said that they were confined to the far north because they could not live in the heat of the warmer climates. They too needed night time to be active, but they wished that the land could be raised in the warmer climes, to allow them to enjoy the coolness that high elevations would bring, and still be able to migrate to the lower lands if the weather got to cold and harsh.

Brother Deer spoke next. He said that it was the purpose of his Nation, as well as that of the Antelope and Elk, to be food for the two legged, and if they were confined to the snowy northlands, it would be hard for them to provide food for the two leggeds who lived in the warmer climes.

Many animals spoke in Council at this meeting. Some spoke of the need for the darkness of night. Others said it was more important that the Earth have high places so the animal nations could spread out and keep their covenants with the two leggeds.

The Creator, in His perfect knowledge and understanding wanted to keep peace and harmony among the creatures. He had a solution that would please them all, and make the earth a more beautiful place.

First, He took the largest moon, and held her in his hands, and proclaimed her the Grandmother of all creation. She was the largest and the brightest, and told the animals that once a month she would come to give them light in their nights. This was to remind them that no matter how dark their darkest nights might be, the light of Grandmother moon would return, just as His love would in her rays.

He then called the "Great Hunter" from his place in the constellations of the Great Star Nation, along with the Thunderbeings to his side. He told them that Grandmother Moon was declared Sacred, and not to be hunted, but they were to shoot down all of the other moons, with their fragments falling to earth gently in places where nothing yet lived. The fragments would create high places to be called mountains. They would provide high places for the Eagle to nest. Cool areas in the southern climes for the furbearers to dwell and keep their covenants. Further, the removal of the many other moons would let the soothing and calming darkness come to the earth, and let the owl and the other night creatures hunt and provide for their own.

The Great Hunter and the Thunderbeings did their work with great skill. They shot their arrows straight and true. The animals watched and cheered as the Earth was remade with the beauty that the mountains brought to it. When the shooting was over, the Earth took on a more majestic look all over. Many flatlands remained for the creatures that loved them. All over the

Earth were majestic mountain ranges for the people and creatures of all nations. The furbearers moved southward and spread out over the earth to provide food for the people. The Eagles began to build their nests in the high rocks and alpine forests that quickly grew in the new richness of the mountain regions.

When the sun went down, the night was dark for the creatures of the night to live as they wanted. The stars could now be seen. The people and the animal nations could now contemplate their place in the vast universe, for they could, for the first time, see it all now. Great joy was found in this new awareness. New songs were sung by the creatures. The insects came alive with their music, and the magic of night was greatly enhanced and savored. Coyotee and his cousin the Wolf howled at the moon, singing their praises to Her, as they do to this day. Brother Owl happily hooted, and became wiser under the canopy of the Great Star Nation."

Thunderbeings

A young Indian man, named John Wolf, walked into a roadside bar and grill in Northern Colorado to have supper after driving all day.   It was getting quite dark, and thunderstorms were rolling through the area. He found an empty table alongside the wall to the left as he walked in. He did not notice any of the people in the place, but he saw mounted animal heads hanging all over the walls, and noticed the smell of spilled beer and cigarette smoke
.

Before he could even take off his hat and coat, a waitress stepped up and asked,
"What can I get ya, Cowboy?"

He pulled off his old hat, which revealed long black hair, with a couple feathers woven into it. He took off his coat and laid it on the chair next to him, giving view to his buckskin vest with his Tribal colors and insignia. He sat down, and said,
"Please give me two hamburgers with everything, and the largest glass of ice tea you

have, Miss," with a smile.

"Coming right up, Chief," she replied.

A rather large man in a cowboy hat, walked up to his table, and slammed a beer down on it, splashing John in the face and all over the front of him.

"Injun," the man said, "you are not in a place where you are welcome. Maybe you better mosey on outta here before you are sorry you came in."

John pulled out his clean hankie, and wiped his face, with many patrons of the place watching,

"Please do not let my presence here vex you, Cowboy. I am only here for a quick bite, and I will be on my way to Cheyenne, to be with my dying mother. I want no trouble, just a quick bite, I have been driving all day."

"Apparently you do not understand English, Tonto," said the big man as he sat down at John's table. "You talk pretty confidant for a man who is alone in a strange place."

"Alone? I am never alone." John grabbed the feathers in his hair. "This is my brother the

Eagle, and this is my brother the Red Tail Hawk."

He then pulled out his necklace, and showed a large tooth next to a claw.

"This is my brother the Wolf, and this is my brother the Puma. And behind you, hanging on the wall is my brother the bear."

"And up above us, always watching over me are the Thunderbeings."

John had been watching the lightning, and counting the seconds till the thunder could be heard. He put his hands up in the air, as if grabbing a rope, and pulled them down with a loud scream. Thunder shook the whole bar, and frightened everyone but John. The bear's head that was hanging on the wall behind the big man came crashing to the floor. It scared the scruff off the big cowboy when it hit his right shoulder and fell on the floor behind him. Every eye in the place was on them now.

"I am never alone, my friend," said John with a slight smile.

The big cowboy just sat there with eyes and mouth wide open.

"Now, my friend," John said, "You want to beat me up because I am different than you. Let me tell you something about the way of my people. I do not fight for fun or amusement. If you want to fight me, I will walk away. If you come after me, I will run away, and if you catch me, I will do everything I can to kill you."

"Who said anything about killing?" asked the big cowboy, "I just wanna whup yer ass and teach a lesson".

"Listen to me, Cowpoke, and then let your actions speak for you!"

"It may be my path, to die in a parking lot at the hands of a white man blinded by hatred outside this Colorado bar. If that is the case, I will accept it, and honor my People as I pass over."

"Or.........and think about this, my friend.............it may be YOUR path to die at the hands of a Red Man who is defending himself from attack."

The waitress brought John his dinner, the big cowboy went back to his seat at the bar. In a little over an hour, John was safely at the bedside of his dying mother in Cheyenne.

14

Grandfather's Letter

Andawehi,
When you walk down that aisle tonight,
and get your diploma, you are beginning your life as an adult in this world.

Please always know how special you are, the only daughter in a family of 13 children. You were sent here to brighten the lives of all who know you. The true strength in the Indian Culture lies in its women. You will personify that strength. You will walk the Red Road in strength, for yourself and for all Red People. You will show understanding and compassion, and not harbor ill feelings towards other people for a past that you, nor they, were not part of. We all must ride the horse that our Father gave to us. You were not given a horse of the 1800s or 1700s. You were given a horse of the 1900s, where the war's of our people will not be fought with arms and arrows. They will be fought with the power of the Great Spirit for the good of all mankind. History has shown that neither men nor mankind can accept one another on their own, therefore the Great Love and Power of the One Creator who made us all will be needed to bring about the union and brotherhood of all people. You will be a leader in this cause. You will represent the Red People proudly and honorably, and help bring about the Brotherhood of all People that the Spirit of all People looks for.

It is an exciting time you are growing into. A time of much turmoil, and a time that the opportunities will come as never before for the Great Spirit to be welcomed into the hearts of all men. At times it will seem to you like you are the only one who is working toward this, but never be discouraged. It is a Silent Walk, and often a lonely one. All men will sit in Council some day, Red, White, Black and Yellow, and the Love of the Great Spirit will remove the word "color" from the language of all men.

A baby step for you tonight, and a long road ahead of you. Your grandmother and I will always be at your side, whether on this side or the other.
Grandfather

15

Keeper of the Ways

The Creator Spirit came to the place of passings and crossings, that netherworld where Spirits checked in from their earthly sojourns, and other Spirits prepare for their entry into the physical world. The faces of those returning displayed every emotion imaginable. Some appeared as if they had just come home refreshed from a wonderful vacation, others as if they were returning from a place of torture and pain. Some, even had the look as if they were not returning from, or to anything like they felt nothing more than ambivalence toward their surroundings.

The Creator greeted everyone, and welcomed them Home, and kept on moving to the area where souls departed.

There was a group leaving to join the Bear Clan. Among these was a restless Spirit who was not in touch with the honor of belonging to this clan,

Many times before this Spirit had been given the gift of being Indian, and had never appreciated what this noble heritage offered him. He had avoided his family and people, and had found little kinship with his animal, plant, and mineral brothers and sisters. And perhaps, most important of all, he had shunned the kinship with the Great Spirit that his heritage and birth right had offered him. The Creator, loving everyone the same, wished to bring into reality for this Spirit the acknowledgment and acceptance of the many gifts that were granted to the People.

This wayward Spirit, known as Shadow Dweller, enjoyed the company of a Spirit Companion, a Spirit named Keeper of the Ways. They had been together many times, with Keeper of the Ways the one who always seemed to spend most of her time, trying to "Keep" Shadow Dweller on a course of growth and learning. The efforts of Keeper of the Ways often were for naught, for Shadow Dweller had a program of his own, and seemed so unworthy of her affection and care. And it was at this time, the Creator placed Its attention on Shadow Dweller, and said

"Come with me."

"I can't.........Keeper of the Ways and I are leaving shortly to join the Bear Clan, and I want to be with her"

"My Son, you are not worthy of lacing Keeper's moccasins, based on the way you have treated her in the past, to say nothing of your people, or Me."

"But Father," cried Keeper, "I do not complain, Shadow Dweller and I have walked many paths, and while I know his actions often hurt you and I both, I need him, I feel it is my mission to help him become what he is."

"My daughter, it is his mission to become what he is, and yours to become what you are. You have not taken enough time for yourself, the self nurturing that all must do, for you have been too busy trying to right the wrongs of one who does not care"

Then the Creator looked at Shadow Dweller and said,

"The free ride is over, My son, you will hear the Voice within you..........you will dance to its music, not that of your earthly ego............you will struggle to find yourself. And the trials that you have avoided in the past, will be thrust upon you in a crash course of what could have been learned much more pleasantly, had you cared to earlier. The choice is always yours, as it is Keeper's.........learn your lessons well, and you will be reunited with her, if it is her desire to be reunited with you. Stay on your present path of stagnation, and never again will you look in her eyes, or those of her people as a friend."

"But father, do you mean I will not be with her or our People?", Shadow Dweller asked.

"My son," the Creator said softly, "you have chosen not to learn from them so far, why should I expect any change in you? You will be born into a white family, far away from the Indian ways that you have taken for granted and spat upon. You will be immersed in ways which are foreign to you, and you will long for the Spirituality and traditions that are part of you, yet kept hidden. Time will reveal if you wish to work your way back, to what has been so freely given you, yet shunned"

Then he again turned to Keeper of the Ways, and said,

"Take this time to be kind to yourself, and polish your skills of tolerance, peace and Love. Just a little fine tuning here and there, and you will be where you wish to be. There are trials ahead for you also, trials you could not face with Shadow Dweller tagging along behind you. It is to be seen, if you can handle your trials, for they will be many and difficult, and if Shadow Dweller can handle his, and if you two will ever be together again"

"Both of you, learn your lessons well, and it is my word that you shall be together again, if you are worthy of such a reunion."

16

Silence

Grandfather broke his silence by speaking *about its treasure to us all.*
"Silence is all we need in order to hear the voice of the Creator. Silence is the buckskin on which the Creator paints His thoughts and wishes for us. Silence illuminates the colors in His voice. Silence disperses the mists that cloud our visions. The most sacred of all spaces on earth is anywhere a man can sit in silence and listen to the dialogue of Spirit."

"The beautiful places in nature call us to

silence. Mother Earth's beauty brings us to that state of mind where we look beyond the body that walks in our moccasins and consider the Spirit that animates that body. We must always take time for silence in our lives, for only after deep thought does the tongue and the mind work in harmony with the Spirit."

"Silence is the body, mind, and Spirit at peace with each other, and the world they live in. To the silent man we give trust. The man who speaks with ready words and little hesitation is not taken seriously. When I was a child, my mother taught me to hold my breath, that I might hear the Hawk sing in the sky. I would listen to the songs of the animals, and in silence take in the life in the forest. The ever changing clouds overhead, the water dancing on the rocks of a stream, all of these things brought wonder to a young boy in reflective contemplation. It was from these silent moments that the loving hand of our Creator was first felt on my shoulder."

"To our Ancestors, the Churches, Cathedrals and Basilica's were spaces in our hearts, not physical structures. Silence opens up these spaces and allows the voice of the Creator to be heard. All we need is the sun rising, the wind making the lush grasses dance, or the moon casting a halo on the world around us."

"To our People, the Turtle teaches us much. Our Spirituality can be compared to the turtle. The turtle needs no external structure for him to live his life. He is self contained. We see our spiritual existence in the same way. We have everything that we need at all times. We just need to silence ourselves, and let the Spirit flow through us, speak to us, sing to us.

"The little ones must know these things, Andawehi, as well as those who have strayed off the Red Road and might need reason to return. There are also many people of other races who wish to learn of us. Through all of the trials and heartbreak that our people have suffered, we have survived, and our Spirit is strong. It is growing stronger and stronger, as the prophecies have foretold. The Circle of Life has never stopped revolving. These Ways which you are commanded to keep shall be offered and shared with all true hearts who seek peace."

*"Their ways are not our ways. We kept the laws,
and lived our religion. We have never been able to understand the white man, who fools nobody but himself."*

Plenty Coups

17

Dawn of the Darkening Sun

Spotted Deer, the Uku, or Great High Priest of the Tribe had not slept well during the night. His Spirit was restless, for he was being given premonitions of something important that was to occur. He knew it was not grave, such as an attack by others, but it was a message to come, through an act he was not familiar with. He knew if he did not fully understand it yet, the People of his tribe would be hard pressed to understand him, as they turned to him for guidance.

He arose at the first sign of approaching daylight, after his meditations and prayers, and left for a walk around the Cherokee village. He knew that in the animals he could find insight to his questions, for the same Great Spirit lived and worked through them also. He could not help but notice right away, after leaving his lodge in the cool morning darkness, that the birds were not singing today like they always do. He found confirmation in this. He walked over a hill and stood at the top of it, watching the horses of the tribe. They were active, and appeared agitated. Normally, they were resting, and at peace. As he walked, he would stop, and listen, and hold his breath. An eerie silence pervaded the land this morning.

Spotted Deer walked down to the lake, where the waters were still. The geese, that normally would be flying out to feed in the fields, now were quiet, and resting in the water. Their normal loud social activity could not be heard on this morning. The Red Tail Hawk, who normally sits high in the trees watching for its prey, was roosting on low branches today. Off across the lake, Spotted Dear could see the buffalo moving around, unlike their normal placid behavior at this hour.

The morning sun was starting to reveal itself in the northeastern sky, and not a cloud was to be seen anywhere. He turned and walked back toward his lodge, with concern embracing his every thought. On the way up the hill, Black Crane, his principal assistant met him, and felt the changes all around them.

"Good Morning, Uku, I have come to walk with you, if I may. I, too, feel the uncertainty in the land."

"Black Crane, please call together the Council of Elders, and the Beloved Women. I need all clans represented, for I have a message given me from the Great Spirit."

"Right away, Uku. We will meet you at the Town Council House."

"Wa Do, Black Crane"

The sun was now nearly risen from the horizon, and Spotted Deer gave thanks for another day as he walked to the Town Council House, in the middle of the Town. The eerie silence would not leave his awareness, for he fed his soul on the songs and music of the animal nations.

He took his place at the front of the Town Council. He had not yet finished his prayers, when the room was complete with those he requested.

"Honored and Beloved Council members, and Beloved Women. I bring you here today, for I have received messages, and I wish to advise, and ask the cooperation of the People for their own sake. The land is quiet today, and the behavior of the brothers and sisters of the animal nations is supporting my revelations."

"I wish, for today to be a day of gathering, at the Council Grounds. A day of introspection, meditation, and brother and sisterhood among us all. I ask that each one of us fast, until I am told differently from our Creator. A message is coming from the Great Spirit, I can feel it. I do not know yet what that message is, but I wish all to be there to receive it. No one shall be punished that does not comply with my wishes, it is a request from the Great Spirit that I make."

The temperatures had been in the 90's and 100's now for two weeks. There was no shade on the Council Grounds. Many were wondering why they would be asked to sit out in the hot sun, and some did not do as asked.

After about an hour, over 90% of the People of the town were at the council grounds, praying, giving thanks, and strengthening their friendships. It was noticed, that the sun was looking very strange, even going dimmer. The dreaded heat that they anticipated was not coming. As this continued to happen, more and more turned to prayer. The daylight was like sunrise now, and it was getting darker, so noticeable now was it that those who did not come to the council grounds at the start, were coming in now, frightened and concerned.

Spotted Deer and his Council and Beloved Women went back to the Town Council House and prayed. He had only seen something like this once in his lifetime, when he was a child. He was told that it was the Eagle flying to sit in Council with the Great Spirit that blocked out the sun, seeking messages for the People, and to bring the Great Spirits grace unto them anew. He left the council house, and walked up on the hill overlooking the town. It was now mid morning, but it was dark as the evening, with an eerie light off in the east. No part of the sun was visible now. The stars were visible, the dwelling place of the Great Star Nations. He looked down on the council grounds, and heard many voices crying, and wailing, and songs of faith. He knew in his heart what was happening, and he gave thanks. He stood on the hill, with his face toward the People, and sang as loud as he could. The members of his council came out, and walked up to where he was. The Beloved

Women accompanied them. His song gave out joy, and hope. It was starting to get lighter again.

He told the Council and Beloved Women that he had something to say to everyone, when the sun was back fully visible. After his words, he wanted everyone to participate in a day of Brother and Sisterhood, and for thanksgiving of the life that we all live. The fast shall be over then, and we shall celebrate our new growth into the Love of the Great Spirit.

By the time the sun had fully appeared, the elders had made their way around, and notified everyone of the wishes of Spotted Deer, the Great High Priest. Soon, Spotted Deer was in the center of the Tribal grounds speaking to his people.

"Beloved ones, we just received a very special message for our Creator. The mighty Eagle, the messenger of the Great Spirit flew this morning to sit in Council with Him from whom all life comes. He has returned to us, as has the daylight. He brings us a message, and grace from He who made us."

"My People, we are given the daylight to see the world in which we live, the world in which we

80

temporarily live. We need the light of day to function in this world, to do what must be done, for the good of all, to wash our clothes, to plant our crops, to tend to our stock."

"We are given the darkness of night, to see the Universe in which we live, and to contemplate and understand our place in it. We are not just part of a finite world which has three dimensions, as we see ourselves during the daylight. We are a part of an infinite world that has NON dimensions."

"The mighty Eagle showed us the darkness today, to remind us not to get too caught up in the workings of the world, especially to the point that we lose perception of our place in the Universe, our Soul, our Spirit, to call us to rest, and take time out, and to always remember to do so."

"As a nation, we were scared today, when darkness settled in, in the middle of the morning. Our fears united us. All Glory and Honor to the Great Spirit. The things that we create in the worldly daylight will remain here long after we are gone, but the love and peace we take into our hearts in the contemplative times of the evening when our work is done, shall be a part of us eternally."

The power and the ways were given to us to be passed on to others. To think or do anything else is pure selfishness.
We only keep them and get more by giving them away, and if we do not give them away, we lose them."

Fool's Crow

18

Most Prized Possession

A grandfather explains to a boy his most prized possession, which can never be taken from him.

"My son, there are many things which can be taken from a man. Things he freely offers; things which must be stolen from him, or relinquished under force; and things which he would never give away, if he could help himself."

"We are held accountable for anything that we would take from another man. The physical things that a man possesses are things of the world, and only affect his life in that time. It would not be pleasant to have to account for robbing another man of what his labors have brought him.   But to me, the worst deed to have to account for would be taking from a man what he cannot give you in his hands. To take from him what is a direct gift of our loving Creator, given only to him, as a spark of the Creator's Life Fire.   This being a man's own dignity, self worth, and connection with the Great Spirit."

"When a man is born, instilled within him is all of the Love and Joy that the Creator manifests through Himself. This, next to the breath of life itself, is the most precious gift that the Creator gives us. Each man is a spark of that Great Joy and Love, born to experience and spread that Love through his passions in life on Earth. Basic to all of this, is his self worth, and dignity as a human being. The Creator gives this to all men, regardless of skin color."

"To take a man's horse, or his food, or his moccasins is to take from him a gift that lasts him only the length of his life in that time. To take from him his self worth or dignity, is to take from him a gift from the Creator that is eternal, that is a part of the Soul, and the Soul is timeless, endless, and always living. I do not understand how anyone could want to stand before our Creator and justify the taking of what the Creator gave to another Soul freely for eternity. To do so, is not only top rob another man, it is to rob the Creator."

"You can loose all of your earthly possessions, my son, and if your self worth and dignity is in tact, you live in riches, Spiritual riches which will sustain you always. Death is the great equalizer of Souls. We can only take to the next life what we have freely given away in this one. Make sure that when you die, you have everything you came in with, and a heart fuller and stronger for the love and compassion that it has given away."

"I say this, to answer your questions, my son. It is not for me to judge or worry about what others may have to account for when they stand before the Great Spirit. As a man who has walked this earth, I have many things of my own that I must account for, and my time is much better spent tending to my own debts, than worrying about the debts of others. I pray with everything that I am, that I have never taken from another man his dignity, or self worth as a precious child of the Great Spirit."

"Where a man's body rests, is of little concern, for grass will grow there. But where his Spirit rests, that is a good place to be."

Black Elk

19

A Warrior's Only Fear

When the hour arrives, that I must die,
Be it evening, noon, or morn,
Will I be sadly wondering why,
That ever was I born?

Will I look out through tear filled eyes,
and see no one around,
and draw my final gasping breath,
on cold, damp lonely ground?

Will I find honor where I lie,
and pass in peaceful grace?
Or will the sullen look of alcohol,
Distort my once proud face?

The feathers of my People's love,
Will they adorn my hair?
As my Soul seeks union high above,
With my elders waiting there?

And when I stand before the One,
As my passing finds its start,
Will I speak the words "This I have done"
With pure and honest heart?

Have I enhanced the common good,
Of which we hear His calls?
And helped the cause of brotherhood,
Helped tear down hatred's walls?

Have I been kind to everyone,
Or just those that look like me?
And in the faces of other ones,
The Great Spirit's eyes not see?

Its true, we are the Masters,
Of our Fate and of our Soul,
And now, forever after,
I shall seek this single Goal.

To send prayers on wings on high,
As I arise each Morn,
And pray I never wonder why,
That ever was I born.

20

Granting Power

The cold winter wind was drifting snow in the shadows of the pines, where the birds sought refuge. The snow settled in the quiet places out of the wind's path like stardust falling in the sleepers eyes. Darkness was returning like a dear friend, bringing the quiet hours that await after the sun sets to nourish the contemplative Soul.

As Nanny walked up the path on her way home from school, she saw the light in the window that told her Grandmother was waiting for her. That light in the window spoke to her of her own personal safe harbor of refuge that the ships would see in the lighthouse lights on the nearby Great Lakes. She had a tough day as a freshman at Mackinaw Island High School, and could not wait to talk to Grandmother about it. She lived with Nanny and her parents, the Ojibwa mother of her mother. She saw in her the embodiment of wisdom and peace, in all situations. She could talk with her about things that her made her uncomfortable in the presence of her parents. This was a special time of day for Nanny, when her and Grandmother could be alone.

She walked in the door to the elegant smells of baking and cooking, something Grandmother loved to do. The wonderful, strong smell of cinnamon told her Grandmother had made some of her famous cinnamon rolls

"Hello, Nanny," said Grandmother as she walked into the back room to give Nanny a hug, "How was your day?"

Tears came to Nanny's eyes. When her eyes made direct contact with Grandmother's, the tears turned into a downpour.

"Oh, Nanny, we need to talk. Let's go sit in the living room, dear," said Grandmother, walking with her arm around Nanny.

"Tell me, Nanny, what is wrong."

"Gramma, that boy, Jarrod, told me he didn't want me around him anymore," she spoke with breaking voice, "He said to stay away from him, he likes someone else. And I cared for him so much, I really did."

"Nanny, I know you did, you have told me about him. I am so proud of you that you cared, and that you know how to care. Remember when we went to Sault Ste. Marie last summer, and you saw the deer get hit by the car?"

"Yes."

"You cried then because of why?"

"Because I care for the animals. They are so beautiful."

"And when the Spencer's home burned last winter, you cried, why?"
"Because I care for them, I care for people. You, Momma and Dad have always taught me to care for others, and other things."

"Yes, my Darlin," said Grandmother with a smile. "You cry because you care."

"Let me remind you of something our People have always known. It can be a risky business to care for other people, and other things. In caring, we grant that which we care about the power to cause us pain, and hurt and sadness. If you did not care about Jarrod, you would not be crying over him. If you did not care about the animals, you would not cry when you see a deer killed by a car. If you did not care about other people, the misfortunes of the Spencer family would not have touched you at all. Do you see?"

"Kinda, but then, so if I am gonna care and be loving as you and mom and dad have taught me, then I am going to cry a lot, and be unhappy?"

"Oh Nanny. To care is well worth the risk of tears and sorrow, for the things we care about can bring us great joy. To care for things outside yourself is to don the clothing of the Creator, for without His great care, we would not exist. It is to walk the Path of the Ancients. The Creator calls us to care, and love on another as ourselves, and to care and love the Mother Earth, and all of His creatures here. You just need to learn how caring works, the risks as well as the rewards. When you care, you are granting what you care for the power to cause you pain. But pain is part of life, great growth can come from our pain. Pain experienced and understood and dealt with polishes the rough

92

edges of our Soul, and gives more light to our Spirit."

"So then, the people are right, who say we were put here to suffer pain on Earth?"

"No, my dear, I do not believe they are right. The traditions of our People teach that in the early days, our People did not know of a heaven and hell, good and bad. Life was accepted as it unfolded. Spirituality was a part of everything the people did. Pain was a part of life, a necessary part of life for our Souls to grow. The Creator only gave us good. They did not fear death, for that was as natural as birth. The idea that pain is bad is foreign to our traditions, for it is a part of life. And to not care, is to allow the threads of our Soul to unravel and hasten its death."

"So then, it must be OK to cry, when in pain, Grandma?"

"Yes, Dear One, of course it is. It is cleansing the hurt and pain from you, a little at a time. Thank the Creator everyday for your caring ways. And remember, the power you grant to others can be taken back. You do not have to cry over this young man forever."

"Nanny, there once lived a man who was Chief of the Great Lakota People. He spoke many wise words, and I want to share some with you. Chief Luther Standing Bear said that a man's heart away from nature soon becomes hard, and he knew that a lack of respect for living and growing things, soon leads to a lack of respect for other humans too."

"My dear granddaughter, please, never loose your caring ways. Let the pain from caring for any part of Creation come into your heart, and leave its gifts there, and then vanish. Give it a proper mourning period, and then send it on its way. Great lessons in Spirituality come to those who break the chains of their sorrows."

21

Language of Spirit

The cool fall breeze pushed the smoke of the campfire over toward five generations of American Indian matriarchy. They were sitting there, on the grounds among many campfires, watching the sunset, and awaiting the appearance of the new moon. As the smoke hit their faces, they each prayed, knowing that the smoke would carry their prayers directly to the Great Spirit. The fading red, orange, and yellow light of the sunset gave way to like colors of the campfire. The fire's light made the faces of Silent Wind, Running Water, Owl Feather, Evening Star, and Two Ponies glow. Their ages ran from 96 for Silent Wind, to 11 for Two Ponies.

It was September, and the tribe was celebrating

a monthly festival of the New Moon, the last one before the Great New Moon Festival. This was a time of gathering as common people and families in celebration and thanksgiving. Many native flutes could be heard. Not far away, some were singing as a group. An elder man could be seen singing by himself to people around him, with his arms opened and raised to the sky. There were many ways to give thanks for the coming of a new month, and soon, a new year.

"Big Gramma," asked Two Ponies, "Have our people always had such beautiful music around them?"

"Yes, my dear," replied Silent Wind, "Music is a special language. It is a common language given to all people, that allows them to speak on the Soul level to each other without an interpreter."

"Soul level?", asked Two Ponies?

"Yes, music, if you hear it, and care for it at all, goes directly to your Spirit. It can animate your body, and make you tap your foot, sing along, or even get up and dance. A sad song, like the ones we hear at the funerals of our loved ones, also go directly to your Spirit. They can make you sad, tear up, or even cry."

"Why is this?"

Owl Feather spoke up, and said,

"My dad always told me that a man cannot lie in music. He cannot brag. He cannot patronize you with false words. He cannot give you a song, and then take it back. Promises which can be broken cannot be made with music. Music does not have to be judged and analyzed as words do, so it goes straight to your heart. People who do not understand each other in spoken or written words, can always find a common ground in music. He would tell of his great grandfather telling how, that when they approached another settlement or camp, long before they reached it, they could know the mood of the people by the music they heard. They understood the war drums of another nation, the music of celebration, and the vulnerability of people in sorrow. Complete silence made them very wary."

"Okay, I am beginning to understand, Grama Owl, for my mom sings and hums a lot. And now I know when she is making music, it is OK to ask her questions and things, he he he," said Two Ponies with a laugh.

"Yes, my dear, it is the same thing," said Silent Wind, with her eyes glowing, and laughing also.

"What about music we do not like, Big Gramma?", asked Evening Star.

"Ah, not all music is liked, and taken in, so you tune it out. That we could be so lucky to do it that easily with words we do not like, or words that hurt and deceive us." replied Silent Wind. "We let words that are said to hurt or punish us enter our minds, and we give them life there all to often, and they become negative energy in us. That cannot happen with music, my dear One. The Spirit gives music a place to dwell within us, or discards it abruptly. And we can learn how to treat the words of others the same."

"I love how we always have music at our festivals, and celebrations," said Two Ponies.

Running Water spoke, and said,

"On the tribal level of our people, for us to survive, we have to be united Spiritually. Through our music and dance, Two Ponies, we connect with each other on the Soul level, and become one mighty Spirit. And we take that

Spirit to a higher level than we are accustomed to everyday. As we do this, we truly become One Spirit, for the common good of our people."

"The United States, and all countries have a national anthem. It is the same to all, a song which it is hoped brings together the Spirits of the people to unite as one Spirit with the Spirit of that country, what it stands for."

"When the people are united with music that touches their Souls, the people feel relevant and equal, as well as draw great strength from each other. This is why you will always hear the music of our people when we gather."

"It does not require many words to speak the truth."

Chief Joseph

"Peace........comes within the souls of men when they realize their relationship, their oneness, with the universes and all of its powers, and
when they realize that at the enter of the Universe dwells Wakan-Tanka, (Great Spirit), and that this center is really everywhere, it is within each of us."

Black Elk

22

The Elder and the Kid

An Elder walked down a sidewalk in a small rural village. He did not get into town very often, so it was a treat for him to do so. After he took care of his business in town, he loved to walk around the shady streets and just talk to people. On this day, the sun was especially bright, and a warm, dry breeze made the outdoors so enjoyable. The shadows were starting to crawl across the lawns and streets. He walked many blocks around this small community.

As he walked toward the town cemetery to reminisce with departed ones, he spotted a young boy, sitting on the steps of a church that belonged to the local Indian Community. The boy looked troubled, so he walked up beside him, and sat down.

"Hello, young man, is this your Church?"

"Yes it is, who are you?

"I am John Whitehawk, an member of your tribe, this is my Church too."

"I don't know if I have seen you here, Mister. My name is Oriah."

"You look worried, Oriah, are you OK?"

"Yes, I am just thinking to myself."

"I am a good listener, if you need one, son."

"Well, when I go to church, I am told that our Creator speaks within me. I am afraid he does not speak in me. I ask my mother and father about this. They tell me that the Creator speaks in everyone, but I just do not seem to be able to hear Him. I listen for His voice, but just hear my thoughts."

"And this bothers you, does it?"

"Yes, of course it does, I am afraid there is something wrong with me."

John Whitehawk looked around the neighborhood they were sitting in.

"Let me think about this, son, we have to find out," he said with gleam in his eye, and a smile on his face.

Up the street a little ways from where they were sitting, was a general store. In front of the general store were many boxes of apples, pears, plums, peaches, and many other fresh fruits. The bright red apples were the most visible, the sunlight was hitting them at such an angle that they looked like they were glowing.

"Say, Oriah, how would you like one of those luscious looking red apples over in front of the general store?"

"I am hungry, I would love one, but I do not have enough money on me. I already looked at them, they are 25 cents."

Now John Whitehawk's eyes really started to twinkle.

"Oriah, no one is around, just run up there and grab one, I will not tell."

Oriah looked up the street for a few seconds, then his eyebrows raised and his head snapped back around and he looked at John.

"John Whitehawk, you cannot be a member of my tribe, or any church, if you think it is ok to steal. I don't think I want to talk to you anymore, I am leaving."

"Wait, Oriah, please," John said as he reached into his grocery bag and brought out two of those beautiful apples. Oriah stopped and turned around, and John offered him the biggest apple.

"You really did not want me to steal an apple, did you John Whitehawk?"

"Let me ask you a question first, then I will answer yours, Oriah. Why did you not go steal one?"

"Because it is wrong to steal."

"But you thought about it for a few moments, what made you stop?"

"Something inside me told me it was wrong."
"A voice perhaps?", asked John with a wide grin, as he bit into his apple.
"Yes, John Whitehawk, a voice," said Oriah as he leaned over and gave John a big hug.

23

Gown of the Soul

A warrior Spirit quietly made its way to a return to the Great Spirit. His death had come suddenly, and quite unexpectedly. Although he had been in many battles, and conducted himself quite honorably, his death came in a moment of shame for such a former noble warrior. He was found all by himself, in a ditch along a deserted trail, frozen in a position that gave away his state of mind when he fell. Like many of us, he had battled alcoholism, but never with the conviction and valor that he battled for his people. His Spirit was strong for the good of his people, but weak for the good of his Soul.

As he journeyed from the physical to the Spiritual, he was accompanied by his Spirit guide, the Coyote. The Coyote traveled alongside its guided one, with head and tail down, as if mourning, which it was. The Coyote teaches the balance of Wisdom and folly, and how they go hand in hand for a successful life. Unfortunately, the warrior did not learn the lessons of his guide as well as he should have, for outside of battle, his life seemed to be pointed toward folly, more than the wisdom he knew and used in battle. Coyote taught him to be playful and have fun. He taught him to be skillful, and adept at the task at hand. He also taught him the craftiness of using the skills of others for the warrior's good... But, Warrior did not learn the balance required in all of the Coyote's lessons. He learned the lessons, but missed the message.

They reached the presence of the Creator Spirit, in a way and force he had never experienced. Pure Love, and energy flowed from the Great Mystery, and a great sense of humility overcame this rebellious Spirit as he came into the presence of All that Is. Warrior and Coyote both knelt in this Loving Presence.

"Son, your work on earth is over, and you have returned Home. Welcome, My Son", said the Great Spirit.

"When you fell, I fell with you. When you

suffered the pain of alienation and scorn that your illness brought you, I suffered also. And when you fought the Great Battles in which you were so brave, I was with you. I never left your side, even though you often turned away from Me, and My Love for you. As you know, I am not here to judge you, only help you account for, and judge yourself, and your actions on earth.

"Are my ancestors here, Great Spirit?" he asked.

"Yes my son, and if you can bear to meet them, you will." replied the Master.

"Bear to meet them? How could I not bear to meet them?" the man asked.

The Great Spirit replied,

"Remember, my son, the time of illusion and deception is over, you are in a pure place, where nothing is hidden. You will see your self, and what you truly added to life on earth, yours and those around you, as well as what you took away, and the pain you caused. Without this knowledge, as painful as it may be, your Soul will stagnate. It may stagnate anyway, the choice is always yours, My son."

"But I was a hero, a warrior of great renown. I fought bravely and courageously for my people, and returned to them," the warrior said in self pride. "I did not die in battle as many of my brothers did, I survived, a true hero to my people!"

"So you say, My Son," the Creator said in a voice of amusement. "Look to your left, at that huge flat rock standing on edge. Open your heart, and let me show you something, and you be the judge, OK?"

"Sure Father," said the warrior Spirit with great self pride, as if he was preparing for more honors.

In the rock, he saw a battlefield, and saw himself riding his horse, fighting bravely. Then behind him in the scene, he saw his most beloved brother fall to the bullets of an enemy. The pride he felt when watching himself ride gallantly on his horse, dwindled quickly as he relived the death of his dear brother.

"That is awful, Father, having to watch my brother die again, why would you make me see and feel all
that I felt then," questioned the teary eyed warrior Spirit.

"But my son, the story is far from over, please turn again to the rock," asked the Father gently.

In this first scene, he saw the village that was his home. He saw elders shivering, for lack of warm blankets. He saw his dead brother's wife out in the dark looking for firewood, as her children huddled together around a dying fire, in clothing that would be honored to be called rags, with the wind blowing through tears in the covering of their tipi. There were horses in this scene, malnourished, and growing weaker from the cold winter. Many were struggling to help each other out, but he did not see himself in this scene. In the next scene, the warrior Spirit saw a body lying in the snow, frozen, with a bottle nearly empty in its hands.

The scene zoomed in, and he saw his own face, frozen in the stare of a slow painful death. He tried to look away, but found he was powerless to do so, and for the first time in the awareness of this warrior Spirit, he knew he was before a Power much greater than his own.

"And you see yourself as a great warrior, do you not?" asked the Father?

The warrior just looked down, crying profusely, in sorrow he had never known.

"My son, in the beginning of that scene you were the great warrior, but did you die like one, as in the ending? Is a warrior just one who kills and fights, and then gives up the Warrior Spirit after the battle is over? Judge for yourself, if you are a great warrior or not, my son. You helped your people greatly in battle, but it appears that you turned your back on them, when you could have helped them the most. Judge for yourself, if you are a great warrior or not, my son."

Through teary eyes, he asked the Father,

"Are you going to send me to the place that

the white man calls Hell?"

"My son, you have just returned from there, a Hell you created for yourself.   Your actions created it, and you chose to dwell in the results of your actions, until you could take it no more."

"What about my mother?", asked the sobbing warrior, "I really need to see her now."

"As you wish, my son," said the Father softly, "behind you, you will see her in the Gown of her Soul, as you have never seen her before. Are you sure you are ready?"

The warrior slowly turned around, and saw the beauty of his mom, oblivious to his presence, but standing near a waterfall. Her hair was long and radiantly black, glistening in the sunlight. Her reddish complexion was like that of the setting sun, so beautiful was she. He could not take his eyes off the beauty of her face, with her hair blowing in the warm, soft breeze. When he left her face, horror filled his heart, as he saw blood spots all over her flowing gown. In terror, he cried out to the Father,

"What is all that blood on the beautiful gown of her Soul?"

"You   do not know, great warrior?" the Creator asked?

"No, and it kills me to see her like this, how could you let this happen to such a beautiful Lady? What kind of place is this?" he cried.

"Do these words sound familiar, my son?"

asked the Father,

"Remember, my son, the time of illusion and deception is over, you are in a pure place, where nothing is hidden. You will see yourself, and what you truly added to life on earth, yours and those around you, as well as what you took away, and the pain you caused. Without this knowledge, as painful as it may be, your Soul will stagnate. It may stagnate anyway, the choice is always yours, My son."

"The blood on your mothers Soul gown is your blood, the blood of the pain and mistreatment that you gave to her. She loved, and still loves you dearly, my son, and she tried with everything she had, to help you understand her love, and she forgave you for the way you treated her. And if you had listened, and accepted her unselfish love for you, and made peace with your beautiful mother before she passed over, her gown would be white, and she would be smiling at you. But, as you can see, as you sit there crying and sobbing in agony over your treatment of her, you are not yet ready to face her in honesty, without illusion, or deception. When you are ready, and are able to stand before her in innocence, respect, and humbleness, you will be reunited with her, and not until then. She has forgiven you, but you have not forgiven yourself."

"Father, how many more have I wronged,

and not treated as you would have had me teat them?", he asked.

"You really want to see all of that now? Or do you wish to begin your work on reuniting with the two people you loved most on earth, your mother and your brother? You have been shown the way, and as always, the choice is yours, my son. The journey before you is long, and will be painful, but the rewards will be yours for eternity, should you choose to take this journey. And should you not choose to take it, to stagnate in the mess you are in now, the pain and sorrow will be yours for eternity also, much harsher than what you have experienced here before me, or worried about finding in the white man's "Hell."

"And as always, my son, the choice is yours"

24

Weeds in her path

The shadows were getting long on this mid October afternoon in the small Michigan town of East Tawas. The fall frosts had called one of its citizens, Mr. John Baker home to his eternal rest. The funeral, which had just ended, called his son Rob and his wife Jean back to East Tawas. They lived in Maine, and had not been back home in over two years.

After the committal service at graveside, Rob told the preacher he wanted to be alone. He and his wife were flying back to Maine the next morning, and he needed the quiet time to gather his thoughts, and reflect on his life with his father, and his life in that small community.

It was a beautiful late afternoon, with the rich hues of the season everywhere to be seen. The breeze was warm, and the songs of the birds brought the cemetery alive. Rob grabbed Jean's hand, and asked her to go for a walk with him.

"In the cemetery?", she asked.

"Yes, this is where all of my people are now. A cemetery is like a library, a history book of the people of an area. As a child, I would come here on nice days, and read the stones, and let my mind be taken on many wonderful journeys. I read about the American Indians and their Sacred Ground, and I think that this is probably as close as us white people have to a Sacred Ground."

They walked among the crimson and fire colored trees. Rob showed Jean the graves of his grandparents. As they left the graves of his paternal grandparents, Rob caught his foot on a headstone, and almost tripped. He looked down at it, and when he read the name he said,

"Oh my God, yes, this is the grave of Mrs. Cotter."

"Mrs. Cotter?", asked Jean. "Is she a relative?"

"No, honey."

"Is she someone who touched you in some way?"

"Yes, she sure did, and I never really knew her, but after her death, she left a lasting impression in my heart. Let's sit down Hon, and I will tell you about her."

"Mrs. Cotter was an Indian lady, American Indian. It is said that her husband, who had roots in this town, brought her home with him after he got out of the service. About a year after they settled in here, he was killed in a car accident. She stayed here, with no family and all. She was a quiet lady but always friendly and pleasant, my mom told me. There was always a light burning in her kitchen, and a faint one in her living room making her home look kinda eerie. The yard was not mowed or taken care of . The house needed painting, and vines grew over some of the windows. The yard was all weeds, except for the small path she made out to the street when she went up town to get groceries or do her business."

"Anyway, I was about 5 years old, just starting kindergarten, in 1954. On the way to school each day I had to walk by her house. Sometimes she would rap on the window and wave at us kids. The older kids told me she was a witch, and to stay away from her. So when ever I walked by her house alone, I would look across the street always, and never at her rundown house."

"My babysitter Ann knew her, and one day her and I were walking by Mrs. Cotter's house. She invited Ann and I into have a jelly sandwich. I was terrified. I was sure I was gonna get poisoned and die that night. Hansel and Gretl kept going through my mind, I guess. Ann enjoyed the sandwich and I tolerated mine, out of politeness. I noticed when I got close to Mrs. Cotter, that she had a mustache. That did it, I had never seen a woman with a mustache before. She had to be a witch, she looked so much different from the white people in our town."

"One day, in the early summer, Ann told me that Mrs. Cotter died. I felt relieved as a kid in my role as Hansel, but I felt sad too, for Ann was teary eyed, and I respected her greatly. I knew if Mrs. Cotter was liked by Ann, she must be OK."

"A day or so later, before the funeral, and at my request, Ann walked me down to the funeral home, and I asked to see Mrs. Cotter one morning. We were welcomed in by the wife of the funeral director, as she put down her vacuum cleaner, and showed me to where Mrs. Cotter lie in state. I looked at her from a distance. It was strange, the smile was gone from her face. I had never seen her without her smile. I walked up closer to her. Her gray hair was long and braided, and laying down her side. She looked very Indian, and very much at peace. I took with me a wondering about the Mystery of Death, which is with me still."

"Mrs. Cotter was buried, and life went on."

"When I started school the next fall, I walked by her house, no fears, no nothing. I looked at the house, still needed paint, vines still growing over windows, and then it struck me. There was no path! Weeds had grown and filled in the path Mrs. Cotter made. More than anything else, those weeds spoke volumes to my young heart about the passing of this woman from this life. I did feel much sadness then."

"I wondered to myself, even then, is that all her life meant, was to make a path in which weeds would grow after her passing? The weeds not only told me she had passed, but also told me that she had lived! She could have planted beautiful gardens, and they could not have spoken louder to me than did the weeds in her path."

"And now, in adult life, I think of her, and the message she left me, and I truly wonder if anyone will notice weeds growing in the path that I leave after I am gone. And even more so, am I even making a path which will give life to anything, or in which anything will choose to grow?"

"You might as well expect the rivers to run backward as that any man who was born a free man should be contented when penned up and denied liberty."

Chief Joseph

25

Waterfall Magic

After a pleasant lunch, Andawehi and Grandfather were back in their car on I-70. At the east end of Vail, Grandfather spotted a very high waterfall, dropping hundreds of feet of the top of a mountain cliff. He asked Andawehi to please stop the car, so he could meditate on the beauty of this work of the Great Spirit's hands. Andawehi pulled the car over with pleasure. Grandfather had slipped back into his reverence for the land around him. She welcomed the peace he found in the land, and loved to listen to his musings. They got out of the car, and sat on the banks of the Gore River, which was fed by this waterfall.

"Behold the beauty. Please let me sit here in silence for awhile."

"I will do the same, Eduda."

Grandfather silenced his mind and went to prayer,
"Great Spirit, I stop now to show You my love for Your Great Works. I stop to listen to the Teacher in the waterfall, to let its medicine fall on me, and give me peace. When I take time to see and hear the beauty in the natural world around me, you give me lessons in Spirituality and Your Love that no book can teach me. We are part of all of this, never separate by design, only by choice when we choose to separate ourselves from Your Great Love."

"My heart will beat longer for having taken the time to feel the energy of this waterfall, to listen to its music, and to give honor to You who created it. You send to us many great lessons in Spirituality that are not found in books, they are found everywhere we look, in Your works, Mighty Creator."

Grandfather continued his silence, and stared up at the waterfall and the skies.

Andawehi saw the smile in his look, and she knew that he was staying true and near the teachings he had always held dear. In her own words, and her own way, she to gave thanks. Being with grandfather like this was a wonderful time for her. Around the ranch, there was always something to do, a fence that needed mending, a tractor that needed repair, or some kind of work to be done that kept them from regularly enjoying time like this. His presence with her was so healing in a time she needed it. His outlook on life and the manner in which he shared his wisdom with her made these moments golden.

Soon, they were back in the car. Grandfather said little, his eyes searching all around the mountainsides, taking in all he could of the alpine land. As they drove up Vail Pass Andawehi said,

"You really love the wilderness, don't you grandfather?"

"Wilderness? This is far more inviting to my spirit than the cement streets of the cities. It is the cities that are the wilderness, where people attack each other like rabid animals. The cities have few, if any, quiet places where the songs of the birds can be heard. They hold few places of natural beauty, for everything is ripped out to create the city. As Cherokee People, we seek harmony with everything in nature. Yes, we ride along in cars made by modern society, drive over super highways that bring us to these beautiful places, and enjoy many good things that the modern society has brought us. But when it comes to Spirituality and advancing our Souls closer to the dwelling place of the Great Spirit, I doubt if we are any farther along on that path than my grandparents were who knew nothing of such modern things. And I truly wonder about my grandchildren and great grandchildren, if they will ever know this peace and understanding?"

"Will they ever know the peace and understanding that you have, grandfather? That is a great concern of mine," asked Andawehi.

"Andawehi, the gadgets and creations of modern society are not bad, for what difference does it make if we step down off a horse, or stop a car and get out of it to feel and give thanks for the beauty around us? The value to the Soul is in doing it, not in what you rode to the beautiful place on. Living and keeping the old ways does not mean we have to live like people did hundreds of years ago. We can live in a comfortable home, and still pray in the direction of the Eagle each evening. The Great Spirit hears prayers from a square home just as well as He does a Tipi. It is not the dwelling place that matters, it is that we take the time to give thanks that matters. That is keeping the ways. It is in seeing the eyes of the Creator in everyone we meet, rather than seeing someone who we can use for our own purposes, or someone who looks and acts different than us. It is seeing and listening to the "teacher" in everyone and everything that was made by the hands of the Creator. It is being true to ourselves, and the Gifts the Creator gave us."

"Always remember that there is nothing all bad, or all good. It is the way we approach things in our life, and react to their presence that determines if they are bad or good for us. I have seen many changes in my life, and I enjoy many comforts I would not have enjoyed had I lived a hundred years ago as an adult. I have always struggled to keep things in perspective. I will find out soon, when I pass over, if I have actions to account for of turning away from the Creator's great Love and Path in order that I might further gain material things. I pray I do not."

*"What is man without the beasts? If all of the
beasts were gone, men would quickly die
from loneliness of Spirit, for whatever
befalls the beasts also befalls man. All of
life is connected.
Whatever happens to the earth, also
happens to the children of the earth. "*

Chief Seattle

26

Classroom Magic

It was early morning at the Reservation school. The children were coming in wearing many beautiful colors of their People. Laughter was heard, as was excited talk about what was on television last night. A little pushing and shoving was going on just to keep things in balance along the way.

Jim SoaringHawk, a third grade teacher, sat at his desk, and smiled as he heard the empty building come alive with the sounds of happy spirits. He loved them all, and his main purpose in life was to teach them and give them a chance as best he could at finding their way. He put down his pencil and set aside his daily planner as children started shuffling into his room. He watched them, one by one, looking into their eyes. He was looking for the shiny eyes of a happy child, and the empty eyes of a troubled one. Today, there was lots of excitement, and it pleased him that none of "his" children looked troubled.

Jim stood up, and the children hurriedly got to their seats. All was quiet now.

"Good Morning, my friends. Welcome back to the place where we all learn, you and I together. It is wonderful to see that you brought so many stars in your eyes this morning."

"Today," Jim said, "I want you to look back with me to the teachings about our ancestors, and the life they lived. Just think about their ways, what they did, and the differences in their lives and ours. And as you do this, think about things in our modern lives that we enjoy, that our ancestors could not. Our lives are different, for sure, but we are still their children, still members of the Indigenous Nations. Please share with the class, as I ask each one of you, the thing that you like most about your life today that our ancestors did not have."

Many hands went up. He knew he had touched something the children had feelings about.

"Della, please tell us what you like about modern

life that our ancestors did not enjoy."

"Television, Mr. Soaring Hawk."

"Okay, good," said Jim with head nodding as if he knew that was coming. "Now tell me what it is that you like about television."

"We can see things we don't get to see. Like magic. Mr. David Copperfield was on TV last night, he did many things, he even made a jet plane disappear."

"I saw that too," said another child.

"So did I," said many others. The room was a buzz.

"Okay, everyone who saw David Copperfield last night please raise their hand," asked Jim.

They all raised their hand. Jim sensed a rare opportunity here to teach the children on a subject that was deep in their culture, his face was alive with ideas. He could not let this chance go by. In his mind, he mapped a departure from his original lesson plans.

"So, magic interests all of you?"

"Yes," came a chorus of voices.

"My dad tells me of my great, great, grandfather who could shapeshift into any animal he wanted to be," said girl in the room.

"My grandmother tells me about the Medicine Man Snow Owl who could sing to rattlesnakes and they would not bite you," said another.

"Okay, Okay," said Jim with a wide smile. Forget about what I asked you to do earlier, today we will talk of magic.

The children clapped their hands and cheered. This was as energetic and excited as he had ever seen them in the classroom.

"There is a big difference in the magic you se on TV, and the Magic of our people. What you se on TV is "illusion". Illusion is making something appear different that what you are really seeing. Illusion usually takes time to set up, and cannot be duplicated right away. Many hours of preparation go into an act like Mr. Copperfield does, and he could not repeat that without many more hours of preparation. And what you see is not what you get, it is entertainment."

"Now, as regards the magic of our people, it is

real, what you see is what you get. You take Jenny's great, great grandfather, one minute he is a man, next minute he is a coyote. And he can do it again and again. And take Snow Owl, that Eric talked about. Every time he sees a rattler, he can sing it to peace, again and again. These men are highly skilled, with much training. The difference is there is no illusion about their magic. Tangible results come from it."

"I wish we could do magic," said Ben. " I want to be like those people."

"Who in here would like to learn magic," asked Jim.

Everyone raised their hands.

"Do any of you feel like you can do magic?"

"Buk can sure make donuts disappear," laughed a girl named Verna. The rest of the room, including Jim, laughed too.

"Put some frybread in front of me, and I can too," said Jim with a smile.

"For our purposes today, Magic is the creation of something from nothing. It is bringing something into existence where it was not in existence before. And you all are people of magic. I am going to show you how you can make magic."

Jim walked around the room with a stern look on his face. The children watched him closely. A boy named Zak was sitting with his head leaning on one arm, with a stern look also. Jim bent down in front of him in the back of the room, so all children could see. He broke out in a very wide, warm smile. So did Zak.

"I just performed magic. Did you see it? I created a smile on Zak's face. I created a smile where there was none before. The forming of a smile is magic, in its purest, simplest sense."

The room suddenly turned to a group of kids looking at each other, frowning, then smiling, and so on. Jim looked at his watch. It was almost 8:30 a.m. when the school administrator, Mrs. Lone Tree was coming to talk to the children for a few minutes about a field trip.

"Kids, please listen to me, we will have more fun with magic. Mrs Lone Tree, the boss around here is coming in a few minutes to speak to us about our field trip next week. Do you see Mrs. Lone Tree as a woman of many smiles?"

"No, you gotta be kidding," was the general reply.

"Okay, no disrespect to her, she has a lot on her mind, and she cares about you very much. But let us use some of our magic on her, all of us will be straight faced till she comes in the room. As she looks at you, everyone do their magic, and I am sure you will see a smile on her face."

The children all laughed and looked forward to this. Jim frowned at them, telling them to keep a straight face. Soon a knock came to the door. Mrs. Lone Tree was asked to come in by Jim, and she turned to look at all the children with that stern look of hers. Thirty eight beautiful, warm smiles greeted her, some with teeth missing, and she could not help but to break out into one herself.

"My, what a beautiful bunch of happy children, Jim. What are you teaching them today?"

Jim motioned his hand toward the children, imploring them to speak.

"Magic, Mrs. Lone Tree," was the reply.

*"Martin Luther King said, "I have a Dream."
But we Indians did not have a dream, we had a reality."*

Ben Black Elk

27

Hawksong

I watched Hawk soar on weathered wings,
Above in cobalt skies,
A messenger of Light and Dreams,
Who calls us all to fly.
I told him he is much revered,
By two leggeds on the ground,
He said, "A Hawk is nothing without,
The Ones the Hawk takes down."

He said, "Do not revere me,
When you see me flying by,
For me to be all I can be,
Little ones must die.
For if you look about you,
You will see them scattered around,
The skeletons and cold remains of,
The Ones the Hawk takes down."

"So when you see me flying high,
And Honor send my way,
Please Honor those who had to die,
That I might live today.

It's true, Hawk is a Noble Bird,
With songs to take around,
But, remember, Hawk in nothing without,
The Ones the Hawk takes down."

*"The old Lakota was wise. He knew that,
man's heart, away from nature, becomes
hard.
He knew that a lack of respect for growing,
living things soon led to a lack of respect
for humans, too."*

Luther Standing Bear

28

Brothers of the Wild

The morning shadows were still long as Chipmunk foraged along an old fence row for acorns. He stayed in those shadows to help hide himself from the many predators of the woods where he lived. He spotted an acorn out away from the fence row and warily walked out to get it. Just as he opened his mouth to take off the top of it, he froze stiff in fear. He could hardly breathe. The shadow he was walking in had moved, and he prepared himself to die at the will of a hungry predator.

Nothing happened. He just stood there waiting for the end to come, and it didn't. The shadow moved again, he knew it was his time. Still, nothing happened. While almost blinded by his fear, he slowly turned around, and looked up to see the mighty Red Tail Hawk sitting on a fence post. The two of them made eye contact, and Chipmunk squeezed his tightly shut knowing for sure he was finished.

"I am not going to harm you, my brother," said Hawk.

"You aren't?" replied Chipmunk.

"The early morning hours have provided great hunting. My family and I have fed well on fresh Cottontail Rabbit.   Right now, I could no more eat you than one of my own."

Chipmunks body loosened up a little, and he opened his eyes to look Hawk in the face. "Are you sure you are not going to harm me?"

"My brother, what did I tell you? We speak through each other's Spirit, not with tongues. Spirit never speaks anything but the truth. It is my good fortune today to be able to enjoy just being a Hawk. To fly for no reason but to feel the air rustle my feathers. To visit with you, my brother, and see you as an sibling heir to the glory and joy of life on earth, an not a food source."

"But you have so much power, skill and strength, I find it hard to believe you do not want to use it on me."

"My brother, all predators have these skills, powers, and strengths. We were given them for one purpose and one purpose only, to enable us to feed ourselves and our families. To use these attributes for any other reason is to break the laws of the Creator's perfect plan."

Chipmunk began to relax, and find comfort in Hawk's words. "My brother, you do not have any predators, do you?"

"Yes, not as many as you, but I must be wary of the presence of Great Horned Owl, and Golden Eagle. They both like the flesh of my kind. We cannot live a decent life when we live in fear of death. We must enjoy our lives, be ourselves, and trust that nothing will happen to us that is not in the Creator's perfect plan, my brother."

"It seems like all I do is hunt for food and sleep. Not really a lot of fun in my life."

"Are there things you would like to do, or you think would be fun doing?"

"Yes, I love to go up by the farmhouse and make the dog freak out. I love to have him chase me, he can never catch me."

"Let me ask you this, my brother," said Hawk, "Had I been hungry, and taken your life for food this morning, would all of that worry over collecting nuts meant anything to you as you drew your last breath?"

"No, of course not, I see your point, Brother Hawk."

"Then go rile up that pooch, guy!" said Hawk with a smile.

The two of them parted with smiles on their faces, Hawk to the skies, and Chipmunk to the dog house.

Chipmunk had a great time, spent the whole day riling up the dog, and then watching the dog get chewed out for barking, and then riling him up some more, and so on, and so on. It was almost dark as he walked home, tired and happy.

Again, he froze, his breathing got tight. He heard the sound of the Great Horned Owl right next to him in the fence row. He closed his eyes

138

tightly. He knew he could not outrun him, so he again, for the second time today prepared to die. Like last time, nothing happened. He waited and waited for the talons to grip him and tear him to shreds. Again, nothing happened.

Again, he slowly turned toward the fence and looked up, right into the wide eyes of Great Horned Owl.

"Aren't you going to take my life and eat me, Great Horned Owl?"

"No, my brother. The early evening provided great hunting. My family and I are fully fed on Red Tail Hawk. To eat you would be like eating one of my own."

" So live your life that the fear of death can never
enter your heart.
Trouble no one about their religion; respect others in
their view, and
Demand that they respect yours. Love your life,
perfect your life,
Beautify all things in your life. Seek to make your life
long and
Its purpose in the service of your people."

"Prepare a noble death song for the day when you go
over the great divide.
Always give a word or a sign of salute when meeting
or passing a friend,
Even a stranger, when in a lonely place. Show respect
to all people and
Bow to none. When you arise in the morning, give
thanks for the food and
For the joy of living. If you see no reason for giving
thanks,
The fault lies only in yourself. Abuse no one and
nothing,
For abuse turns the wise ones to fools and robs the
spirit of its vision."

"When it comes your time to die, be not like those
whose hearts
Are filled with fear of death, so that when their time
comes
They weep and pray for a little more time to live their
lives over again
In a different way. Sing your death song and die like a
hero going home."

Chief Tecumseh

29

The Spirit Tree

As he drove over the mountain pass, Ben Short could see down into the valley that was to be his retirement home, where he would live till Spirit called him to his true home. There was the ranch house, the barns, and the glorious land that rose from the road up into the Big Horn mountains. There were many rock outcroppings among the evergreen trees, as well as a rambling stream down through his property.

Ben bought this property just a month ago, on a vacation. It was love at first sight. He saw the ranch, and he bought it. Something here called him to spend his twilight years here, something told him this was where he belonged. He was moving to the ranch from back east, where he was a Psychology professor at Ohio State

University. For him to come here and live in these beautiful mountains while he was still healthy, was a dream come true.

A couple days later, nearing sunset, as Ben was finishing his supper dishes, Buckeye, his Black Labrador started barking up a storm. Ben did not pay a lot of attention at first, but as it went on, he went outside to see what had Buck's attention. He looked down to the west fence line about a quarter mile away from the house. There were about 7 people walking along the fence, heading north along the west fence. To Ben, they looked like Indian People. He told Buck to hush, and went and got his binoculars to watch them. Through his binoculars, he thought for sure they were Indian. Their dress was quite traditional, with feathers in some of their hair. He watched them walk to the back of the front forty, and then cross the fence onto his land, and walk to the east, and disappear in a grove of trees. This puzzled him, but he did not dare go back there. He, like most white people, did not know very much about the Indian People. And, as is usually the case, what Ben did not understand, he feared.

Early, the next morning, at around sunrise, Buck started barking again, this time in Ben's bedroom. His fears caused him to jump up, and

142

look out the window down to the west fence again. This time, there were about 12 of them walking south along the fence row, coming from the north. He reached for his binoculars, and again saw Indian people in traditional dress. This worried him now, were they doing drugs back there? Were they growing drugs or pot back there? Were they illegally killing animals? Something not good had to be going on back there. He knew there were American Indian People around here, but he did not know what tribe they were. He did know, that he did not like them walking on his property at weird hours.

After breakfast, Ben decided to call Professor Ron Dark Elk, a friend of his who was the head of the Native American Studies Department at Ohio State. Ron was of Lakota descent, and Ben thought maybe he could help him in how to handle this. Ben thought his retirement was getting off to a bad start with strange people running all over his property at will.

Ben caught Ron in his office, and told him what was going on. "Ben, you say they only do this at sun up and sunset?"

"Yes, Ron."

"Ben, you are in the land of the Crow People, a

very strong and Spiritual People. I am catching the next flight to Billings. I will call you on my cell phone before I take off, and tell you what time to come and pick me up at the airport. I must come out there and see this." They exchanged pleasantries, and said Good Bye's for now.

Now Ben was really puzzled. "What was going on?" he asked himself.

Ben got his call from Ron, and at 3:00 p.m. he and Buck were at the Billings airport awaiting Ron's arrival.

When they met, Ron said, "Please do not ask me any questions, let me go to your ranch, and see what I can see. I will explain all of this later. Trust me, my long and dear Kola."

Ron looked as Indian as did the people Ben watched walking the fence row. He did feel a greater sense of comfort having Ron with him. As they came over the hill that revealed the ranch in the valley below, Ron's eyes got real big, and he went into silence, and just stared at the land. They drove down into the valley with neither of them saying a word. When Ben pulled his truck into the driveway of the ranch, Ron had his eyes focused to the back of the property in a grove of trees. He got out of the truck without saying a word, and started walking back to the rising hills that lead up to the Big Horns.

Ron walked into the house after dark, with a peace settling over him like a baby's blanket. "Ben," he asked, "you told me something called you to this ranch, something told you this was home, where you wanted to live until you pass over?"

"Yes, Ron, but now I am not so sure."

"You felt it, and you will feel it more, my brother. This is a very special piece of land."

"What do you mean, how does all of this tie together?"

"Ben, on your land is a Spirit Tree. There are many places in the world where the Great Spirit comes to rest, to watch, to observe and to sense His creation. They can be rock outcroppings, they can be streams or rivers, but yours is a Spirit Tree. The Crow people have been coming to this place for centuries. They mean no harm to you or anyone. They come here when they feel the Great Spirit taking temporary residence in that tree. Some call these places Power or Energy Centers, which they are, for all power and energy is of the Great Spirit."

"But I thought that your people saw the Great Spirit in everything anyway."

"We do, but this is something very special, where the Great Spirit concentrates His energy while he rests, and sees the world He created through the eyes and senses of all of His children here. You could feel this when you came here to buy it, something told you this was good land. When you see the Crow People walking back there, you will know that the Great Spirit has taken residence in that Spirit Tree."

"Knowledge was inherent in everything. The whole world was a library"

Luther Standing Bear

30

Grandma Manyfeathers

An young Indian lady is asked to deliver a eulogy at her grandmother's memorial service. She spoke these words of her grandmother:

"It is because of you that the blood of the First Nations flows in my veins. It is you who nurtured me on my journey down the Red Road and fed my spirit on the wisdom so lovingly given down to you. You taught me that the Red Road is a spiritual road, and to always nurture our Spirits first, for when our Spirits are nourished, and allowed to manifest within us, we can handle anything. You taught me to never let my vanity have more power or voice within me than my Spirit, for vanity keeps us locked into the world and makings of man, and away from the true world of eternal Spirit.

"It is you who taught me to walk barefoot on our Earth Mother, and feel her pulse more than my own. It is you who taught me to feel the winds of the Universe flowing through my hair when the winds of Earth were silent. It is you who taught me to feel the comfort of the Starlight and to let it warm my soul like the noonday sun warms my shoulders. It is you who taught me to see the Creator in all living things, to hold my breath and hear Him sing in the voice of the Eagle. It is you who taught me the brotherhood we have with all living things, the plants, animals, and rocks. In teaching me this, you taught me that a man whose heart turns cold toward nature, often turns cold toward his own kind also. It is you who taught me to see the Tapestry of rich hues in the wind, and to let the four winds paint my Soul with the words and wisdom of the Ancients. It is you who taught me that we breathe the same air as our ancestors, we drink the same water, and that the Great Spirit that lived within them lives within us. You taught me that this is true of those yet to be born, also, and we must take care of what is only ours to use, not own. We must see to it that they have a beautiful Earth to live on as we do.

"I did not love and adore you because you demanded it of me. I was drawn to you through your quiet ways and gentle love, hoping that in following you, I could be more and more like you. You did not beat me over the head with your values and morals, I absorbed them from watching the way you lived your life, handled your frustrations, and accepted your setbacks.

"Grandmother, when my parents died, I remember the preacher saying at their funeral that they now "were free". And I wondered then, as a little 6 year old girl, is life on earth supposed to be bad, so we can finally find freedom when we die? If that was true, why bother? In you, Grandmother, I learned that we are free the moment we are born, and the only one who can make our Spirit strong or weak, happy or sad, is ourselves. The world and all living things within it are beautiful, if we will only open our eyes to that possibility, and not let negativity have any room to grow within us. And for those who did not see much beauty in this world, you taught me to pray.

"Grandmother Manyfeathers, I will always honor your life, and the Great Spirit that dwells within us all, by carrying on your ways, and sharing them, and giving them to Souls yet unborn, as well as those here with me now. Thank You,

Grandmother Manyfeathers, for accepting this halfbreed little girl as your own, and loving and nurturing her in your ways."

"Your nation supposes that we, like the white
people, cannot live without bread, pork, and beer.
But you ought to know that He, the Great Spirit
and Master of Life has provided...........for us in these
spacious lakes........and woody mountains."

Chief Pontiac

31.

Fallen Warrior

Kiwase slowly blinked and opened his eyes
for the first time in hours. The Lakota warrior
was mostly in another world, but gradually
fading back to this one. As his spirit reentered
his earthly body, the silence around him was
deafening. At first he thought he was deaf, for
the sounds of battle could no
 longer be heard. But then a gust of wind
brought coolness to his face, and whispered the
voice of the Great Spirit through the tall
grasses it made sway around him. The more he

returned to consciousness, the more it invoked its spoils, such as the sensation of pain. He found himself too weak to move, with pain in his legs that made him want to scream as loud as he could.

The gust of wind returned just like a friend, and whispered his ancient name Kiwase, and gave him another breath of fresh, cool air. He listened for the sounds of the animals and heard none. He and his brother warriors were taught to speak in the voices and sounds of the animal nations to let each other know where they were. He heard nothing. "Have they all been killed?", he wondered to himself.

As the shadows grew long, and the sun was setting, the breeze occasionally brought with it the stench of death. The day had started out with so much promise, the smell of blooming buds, a relaxed camaraderie among he and his brother warriors, and the birds of the air singing and flying around. What a change the attacking enemy brought, a change that reminded him of the basics of life from which he tried to never stray. He prayed to the Great Spirit,

"Great Spirit, I thank you for the life within me. I thank you for the pleasures I have known in your love.

I thank you for my wonderful wife, and the love
of yours I feel through hers.
I thank you for my two beautiful children, and
the love of yours I feel through theirs.
You know my needs, Great Spirit, as well as
theirs.
I know they all are safe in your love, as I always
have been.
If my path is to meet the Woman in the West,
I am ready.
If I am to stay in this wounded body, and carry
on as your child on Earth,
I will do so with love and pride that Honors you,
Great Spirit.
All glory and honor is yours, Great Spirit."

After prayer, the pain returned in full force.
Through tear filled eyes he looked up at the
reddish skies. He was starting to drift off again,
away from his pain, when he noticed the faces
of departed Elders looking down on him. Their
eyes foretold of concerns.

"Kiwase, arise and walk with us, Son. There is
something here you have been chosen to watch,
and to understand," said one he recognized as
his Great Grandfather Walking Bear. Kiwase left
his body, and rose up to walk with these
Honored Ones.

They looked down across the battlefield. "What do you see, Kiwase?" asked Walking Bear.

"I see the Spirits of friend and foe embracing each other. How can this be when they were just a few hours ago trying to kill each other?"

"Kiwase, they are leaving the influence of a world ruled by ego centered and greedy political entities, and they are returning to the unifying influence of a kind and loving Great Spirit."

"But so soon, Walking Bear, I am amazed."

"Kiwase, this is what the heart of all mankind longs for. The Great Spirit speaks in all men, but those are few that will quiet their tongues so that the He may be heard. The prophecies of our People tell of the day when the earth shall know this harmony, when all men walk as brothers. What you are seeing now from the Spirit side, you will see someday from the world side. Look about you, the four great races of man are embracing each other, after killing each other for a cause they once felt to be worthy. The Red, the Yellow, the Black and the White. Only moments into the world of the Great Spirit, and they see the folly in their ways, they see their old mistakes repeated again. Every time a warrior of any race returns to the Great Spirit

154

after losing his life in a battle, that is likely one less warrior that will act aggressively toward another man in the future."

"It can be seen from this side, and these warriors all see it now, that the blood that stains the rich soil of our earth mother is human blood. No One can tell whether it came from a Red man, a Yellow, Black or White man. Those colors mean nothing over here."

"And as those bodies decay, and return to their Earth Mother from whom they came, the skeletons will be human skeletons. The color of skin that the world so focuses on will be gone."

A smoky white, ivory gate formed to the west of the battlefield. It led to a funnel like cloud that led up into the skies. One by one, the spirits of all the fallen ones, friend and foe began walking toward this gate. Some entered with their arms around another, and some alone. As they entered, they could be seen flying up into the funnel, returning to the darkening land, the land of Spirit, the lands of loving influence of the Great Spirit.

Kiwase turned from Walking Bear, and started walking toward the gate.

"No, my son, it is not your time. We have been sent to tell you this, and to impart medicine to you, that you are to share and help others prepare for.   We have been sent to tell you this, and to give this medicine to you, that you are to share and help others prepare for. You may reenter your body now, help is on the way. We walk with you always, my son."

Kiwase laid back down and reentered his body. The pain again became so unbearable that he passed out.

Kiwase was awakened soon by the sound of helicopters, that shattered the silence of the Viet Nam Central Highlands. He heard a medic shout, "No body bag here, this man is alive!!!!"

32

White Eagle Woman

Thunder Skies awoke before dawn, as was normal for him. After walking down to the river and bathing, he came back into the Tipi and added wood to the fire. He stepped back outside, and marveled at the new surroundings. The village had moved yesterday, providing new vistas for this lover of the Earth to feed his heart on. He looked up into the skies, and saw the universe the same as he always had, with eyes full of wonder, and a humble, thankful heart. There, so close he felt he could touch her, was Grandmother Moon. Thunder Skies held his arms wide apart with hands lifted to the sky, and gave thanks for the wonderful life he lived. This was in the time long before the culture of the Indigenous People was diluted and influenced by cultures from Europe.

The Scout of the tribe had recommended this move, as he had discovered the Buffalo herds were great just over the ridge to the northeast, where the sky was starting to glow.
Today was going to be a day of hunting for the braves, and a day of settling in for the women of the tribe. With a river nearby teeming with fish, Thunder Skies felt like they had discovered paradise, although, truth be known, he felt that way no matter where he walked on Mother Earth. Other men from the tribe walked by him, few words were said, as the day of the hunt was a very serious one, for the food of the tribe was dependent on their success. They would get together soon, and without words being necessary, assemble and ride to the dwelling place of the Honored Buffalo.

Thunder Skies stepped back into the Tipi. Hi face smiled widely, as his wife and Honored Lady, Spring Fawn had risen also. She was preparing food for the morning meal, to give her warrior the energy he needed on the hunt.

"Greetings, Spring Fawn, my love," he said.
"Greetings, Thunder Skies."

He looked at her with teary eyes, teary eyes

of happiness for all of the love he knew since they had been wed a year ago. He was proud to be Lakota, especially for the way women were honored and held in high esteem as the "givers of Life."

Spring Fawn handed Thunder Skies a hearty bowl of food she had prepared. They sat and ate together, speaking few words, but saying much to each other. When they had finished eating, and things were put away, Spring Fawn knelt in the middle of the Tipi and bowed her head. This was one of Thunder Skies' favorite moments of the day. He picked up the Porcupine tail comb he had made for Spring Fawn, and began combing her long black hair. He was carrying on the ways of the Lakota men since time began, that of giving his wife his attention before he went off on his day.

He brushed her hair until it was straight and pretty, and he tied it so if flowed down her back as one strand. After this, she raised her face to him, and he took paints that she had prepared, and painted her face for her day. If she was to be out in the sun all day, he would paint it heavily, and accordingly if she was not. He painted her face heavily today, for she had much to do in settling in to their new surroundings. There was wood to be gathered, things of the land to be picked for food, as well as decorating their Tipi for this new location.

They both were a little startled when suddenly before them stood a tall woman in a robe of white feathers.

"My children, I come to you as the mother Eagle returns to the nest to feed her young. I bring food for your Spirits, that you may fly like the Eagle does."

"Who are you?", asked Spring Fawn.

"It is I, who causes the morning dew to settle on the wings of the butterfly. It is I who sings to you through the song of the Hawk. And it is I who whispers your names in the wind while you steal away to the Dreamlodge."

"Have we offended you?", asked Thunder Skies.

"No, my beloved ones. I see the world through your eyes often. I look through your eyes and see the brightest stars of the skies reflected in each of your eyes. Your love allows you to see these stars, and the beauty within you both. But I am here to tell you that one is coming in whose eyes you will see the soft stars of the Milky Way. You will see an innocence and gentleness that you have not seen before."

"But we do not understand," said Thunder Skies,"at least I do not." Spring Fawn looked at him with a sheepish smile.

"I am sending a child of mine, for you to care for as long as she is there. I cannot tell you how long the ribbons of her laughter will grace your home. I send her so that she may learn from you, and that you may learn from her. She, like you, is a precious child of mine, and no matter what might befall her, my love for her is endless, as it is for you. She will bring you much joy and love, and as a child, remind you much about my ways. Both of you are true followers of your People's path of faith. Remember, the one who is coming is my child, before she ever sets foot on Earth. You are to give her your gifts, and take from her the ones she offers you, one day at a time. And should I call this child home before I call you, you will cling to the golden moments of joy that she brought to you, and not hate me, or turn away from the truths that have sustained your people always."

The Eagle woman vanished, and Thunder Skies and Spring Fawn broke out in tears of joy. As he left to join the others for the hunt, Thunder Skies sang an ancient song of praise and thanksgiving so loud that everyone in the village could hear him.

"Silence meant to the Lakota what it meant to Disraeli when he said, "Silence is the Mother of Truth", for the silent man was ever to be trusted, while the man every ready with speech was never taken seriously."

Chief Luther Standing Bear

33

The Black Owl Trilogy

Part I

Black Owl

His name was Black Owl. He was the most feared man in the Taquahoma Territory by those who chose to make him their enemy. He was the most admired man by those who sought his friendship. He was the youngest man ever to be elevated to War Chief in his tribe. His fearlessness and leadership on the battlefield was legendary among the Indigenous Nations and the United States Army alike.

A couple years ago, Black Owl signed, for his people, the Treaty of Crooked Fork. Like all treaties before it, it amounted to the Indigenous People ceding more of the land they loved to the United States Army, in exchange for peace. This treaty gave the Indian People sovereign rights to the land west of the Crooked Fork River in the Taquahoma Territory. He signed it begrudgingly, having witnessed himself three treaties signed by his people, only to be be transgressed by the Army, in their westward march.

Black Owl declared, the day after signing that treaty, that he would sign no more. His people had given up to much of the land they loved to the bluecoats. He pledged to his people, that as long as he was alive, and he planned on living a long time, that the footprints of United States Army soldiers would never step on the lush land that embraced the graves of his elders.

Since the Treaty of Crooked Fork had been signed, the tribe had enjoyed a rather peaceful life. There were no major battles or intrusions by the United States Army or settlers into the tribal lands. Black Owl was very thankful for this peace, yet wary too, for he knew history well.

Black Owl's wariness was vindicated early one

morning when Swift Eagle, the scout of the tribe , returned from an eastern trip and scratched on Black Owl's lodge and woke him with startling news. The United States Army had sent a platoon of soldiers about five miles west of the Crooked Fork. They had set up a camp on this side of the Widow Hills, about 10 miles away. Black Owl was extremely saddened by this news. He had heard this story all too many times in the past. This intrusion was a clear violation of the Treaty of Crooked Fork.

"It appears, my brother, that a new push is starting for forts and settlements west of the Crooked Fork. Let me walk for a few minutes, and clear my head of the Dream Lodge. When I am thinking clearer, I will be back, and learn more from you."
"Yes, Black Owl, I will wait for you here."

After about 15 or 20 minutes, Black Owl returned.

"What was your impression of the camp?"

"I saw only one platoon there, twenty men, but the way they were setting it up, it looked like more were coming."

"Swift Eagle, you are a man of truth and honor.

165

I would bank my life on your words. Although my heart is terribly sad that it has come to this again, we must assemble our warriors. Please spread my words to the warriors, and the leaders, that we will assemble and leave tonight just after the sun is down.

Ask them that they spend today preparing themselves, and their horses for battle. We will travel under the care of the Great Star Nations, and be ready for battle when the sun lights our path."

Around noon, later that day, a couple of warriors came to Black Owl's lodge to ask him some questions about the days ahead. One of them was Broken Talon, Black Owl's hand picked protégé. They were alarmed when they did not find him home, or his wife and children. This did not seem right at all.

They turned to walk into the village further, and noticed a group of Elders praying and singing the spiritual songs of their people. Strangely they saw few women or children. Broken Talon walked up to one of the Elders and asked,

"Honored Elder, do you know where Black Owl is, and the women and children?"

"Go to the place where the dancing water passes below the Sleeping Bear's nose. You will find them there."

This meant the rapids of the Laughing Fox River at the north end of the Sleeping Bear Hills. Broken Talon was disturbed, that their fierce and brave War Chief was with women and children rather than his warrior's on the day before battle. He had to know why.

As they approached the rapids of the Laughing Fox, they could hear singing and drum playing in celebration. What is going on , celebration the day before war, Broken Talon said to himself.

They got off their horses, and walked down through the poplar trees to view the sandy flats along the river where the celebration was going on. As they did, they noticed many women of the tribe sitting in the trees watching the fun. Black Owl's wife noticed them, smiled at them, and motioned for them to sit and watch.

Through the trees, they could see Black Owl beating on his drum, and they could hear him singing. The children danced and laughed. Any child that was old enough to stand up at all, was out there shaking body with the group. Every so often, Black Owl would stop, and show the children new steps to a new dance, and then play his drum and sing new songs. Sometimes he would ask the children to sing, and he would dance the dances of the People.

The children loved it all, as he would randomly grab them, and give them a hug, and dance with them.

After an hour or so of this, Black Owl opened his leather bag, and gave dried buffalo jerky to the kids for lunch. They drank the fresh water from springs nearby. When they ate their jerky, he gave them each a honey candy his wife made, and a hug, and sent them back to their mothers.

After the children had departed with their mothers, Broken Talon walked down to where Black Owl sat in the sand on the banks of the Laughing Fox.

"Black Owl, what we just watched was beautiful, but on the day before war?"

"My brother, I am a man of peace, our people are people of peace. I find no joy in going to war. It is something we must do to sustain the lives we love, for ourselves, and those to come."

"But Black Owl, white men are lodging on our land. It is said that you hate white men, and that they hate you, yet you frolic with children."

168

Black Owl's eyes turned deep yellow like those of the feathered owl, and Broken Talon felt their piercing burn.

"Broken Talon, do not ever make your tongue rapid with me," said Black Owl sharply.

" Black Owl hates no one, for hatred ties us to that which we despise, and I choose not to be tied to the white man when he cannot keep his word to us. He and I are brothers, children of the Great Spirit, brothers who have yet to find a common ground, and I pray every day that we do."

Broken Talon looked down at the ground, ashamed that he had angered such an honored man.

"Broken Talon, I do not go to war out of hatred. I am going to war because I love my people, and the lives we have lived down through the ages as free people. As for the celebration with the children, I felt the poison of hatred enter my body when Swift Eagle told me of this intrusion. I have seen many battles, way too many faces of death. Even in victory, my heart weeps, knowing my soul is now wearing the blood of those I have killed. Each time we paint our faces for war, I wonder, why must it come to this, what is it lacking in mankind that we cannot just let get along, let everyone live? This land is big enough for everyone. The Great Spirit did not put us all here just to stain the beautiful skin of our Earth Mother with each other's blood."

"I went to be with the children today, for they are the farthest removed from hatred, they have yet to learn it, and I pray they never do. Life is beautiful to the children, they are full of joy and good humor. I want their children to have a chance to love life too. It would do you some good, Broken Talon, to spend time with them."

"Now, be off with you, and prepare yourself to fight because you love your life, and the people you live it with, not because you wish to look into the eyes of a dying man. I am ready for battle, are you?"

34

The Black Owl Trilogy

Part II

Journey to the Battle

The setting sun turned the shadows long as the warrior's gathered at the dance grounds. The warrior's told their loved ones "see you later" in the language of the people, which meant tomorrow, in a few weeks, or in the next life. As they turned and rode to the center of the dance grounds to take their place in formation, they received the blessings and prayers of those they parted with.

Soon the sun was gone and the war party was assembled. Black Owl arose on his his horse and stood on its back to address everyone in prayer,

"O Great Spirit, who so beautifully
manifests your love for us
in the laughter of our children,who
bestows your care
for us in the nurturing hands of our
women,
and who shelters your infinite wisdom in
the hearts
of our elders,we ask you to bring us a
lasting peace, and let a common ground be
found
between my brother the white man and I,
that we no longer find reason to fight and
kill each other,
that all men be free to live the life of their
ancestors
on land that is sacred to them.
Please, Great Spirit, understand us, your
children,
that as we leave for war, we are fighting to
hold
onto something we love and hold very
dear, the
life that our people have lived down
through the ages.
We do not fight to take land from others,
or to
try and force our way of life on a people

**that does
not want it. We fight, and are willing to
die for the existence
that we love, ever mindful of your
presence
within us."**

With that, Black Owl sat down on his horse, and motioned for his warriors to follow him to the east. Riding beside him were Swift Eagle, the wise Scout, and Broken Talon, the understudy. No words were spoken as the journey of hours began. The direction of travel was guided by Swift Eagle, for he was at the site of the encampment the night before. They rode close to the trees as they could, preferring the protection that the forests offered should they be being lured into a trap.

About an hour into their trip, Swift Eagle stopped and pointed out a soft golden glow in the distance. It was the trees reflecting the light of the campfire of the soldiers in the Widow Hills. Black Owl found this strange, that they would choose a campsite where their fire could be seen so far west. He now fully expected to find a large group of soldiers there, and a major battle to come. He said nothing.

About an hour and a half later, Swift Eagle called

the party to stop. He turned to Black Owl and said,

"As you can tell now, the camp is just over the foothill of Widow Hill. That fire is large, I expect many soldiers there."

"As do I, Swift Eagle."

Black Owl turned around, and called to Red Stick, one of his best warriors.

"Red Stick, Swift Eagle, Broken Talon and I are going to ride up and scout the camp. I must see for myself what we are up against, before I can plan our actions. I leave you in charge, and I ask that you let the men rest. Pay close heed to our travels, and should you hear any gunfire, or war chants from either one of us, come up there full strength. Otherwise, rest."

The three of them rode up into the Widow Hills, keeping and eye on the trees glowing from the fire, and the land around them.

"Let's get close. Let's leave our horses here, and walk to the camp," said Black Owl.

They stole through the night, under the Great Star Nations, and arrived on the hill just above

174

the camp. There were no signs that the soldiers had traveled any farther west than their camp. They looked down into the camp partially surrounded by trees, and open to the south and east They counted twenty horses, and twenty soldiers. Black Owl was really confused now.

Black Owl nodded his head, as if he knew something.

Broken Talon asked, "What do you think, Black Owl?"

Black Owl just put his forefinger to his mouth.

"I must see this closer, I am going down into the trees behind the camp. You two stay here." It was not long and Swift Eagle and Broken Talon could hear Black Owl in the trees behind the fire. He was making his trademark owl hoot, telling them he was ok, and spooking the soldiers. No soldier would sleep good after hearing an Owl hoot in the land of Black Owl.

Black Owl surveyed the scene from every angle possible. After about an hour, he returned to Swift Eagle and Broken Talon.

"We can take them, Black Owl, we can wipe them out," said Broken Talon.

Swift Eagle turned his head to keep from laughing out loud at the young man's over zealousness.

"My brother, you listen to me, and you listen good. Our people have not enjoyed the wonderful life we live by spitting in the face of the Great Spirit,"
said Black Owl.

"But I do not understand, Black Owl."

"There are many things you do not understand, and I suggest you shut up, and listen, and reach for a little understanding starting right now!"

"First of all, this is a trap. Learn to read what your eyes see. These are not battle ready soldiers, they are old men sent here by the bluecoats with big hats to provoke us into attacking them. And if we attacked them, and killed them, them they could get permission to come after our village full force, since we wiped out a platoon of their soldiers. We should kill these innocent men and put our village at risk?"

"Secondly, their carelessness. A troop of soldiers over here on business would not build a fire on the east side of the Widow Hills that could almost be seen from our village, to say nothing of being seen 5 miles away in any direction. These men were told to build a huge fire, in hopes it would attract us, and would kill them all.

"Thirdly, the men and the horses. The soldiers have bellies bigger than our women when they bear our children. They were sent out here as "sacrificial lambs" to use a term from their spirituality. Blue Coat wants us to kill these men, and give him an excuse to come after our women and children, and elders. The men are drinking liquor, hardly the style of the United States Army on duty. Their horses are in bad shape, and poorly taken care of. This is hardly and elite fighting corp. To go to battle with these men would shame me greatly, and I would be spitting in the face of the Great Spirit and my Elders who taught me about Him.

Black Owl then asked Swift Eagle to ride to the south to the village of Lame Bear, and ask him to assemble his troops and meet him where the Crooked Fork doubles back on itself. He then asked Broken Talon to ride north to the Village of Running Elk, and ask the same of him.

Swift Eagle thought to himself, as he rode off in the darkness, our warriors, Lame Bear's warriors, and Running Elk's warriors, there will be a thousand warriors there tomorrow morning, what could Black Owl be planning?

"The attitude of the Indian toward death.......Death has no terrors for him; he meets it with simplicity and calm, seeking only an honorable end as his last gift to his family and descendants. Therefore, he courts death in battle; on the other hand, he would consider it disgraceful to be killed in a private quarrel."

Ohiyesa

35

Black Owl Trilogy

Part III

Touching the Enemy

The first hint of daylight found Black Owl and his war party riding east through the morning mist toward the encampment of Army soldiers. He told his warriors little, except that no one was to fire unless fired upon first, or unless he gave the command to fire. He instructed them as always, that if they took prisoners, they were to take no liberties to harm the prisoners. He said every battle offers many chances to learn, about one's self, and about the foe.

When they got to the campsite, the soldiers were asleep. The war party circled the campsite, from the hilltop above, down the hill, and around through the trees back up to the top of the hill. When this was complete, Black Owl walked to the center of the camp, and stood by a sleeping soldier. The youngest warrior's looked on in awe, the older ones accustomed to Black Owl's style of leadership. He took a revolver out of a holster from the soldier near him. Black Owl held it high, opened the gun to show everyone it was full of bullets. He then closed the magazine, and pointed the gun at the soldier's head. He pulled the trigger 6 times, much to the shock of his warriors. Six clicks were all that they heard. The soldier awakened. Black Owl stood on his chest with one foot, and pointed the revolver at him. The soldier froze in horror. Black Owl motioned for his warriors to take each soldier as he had. It was done in a heartbeat. Ravens yacked in the trees to the east of them. A gust of morning breeze made the leaves of the poplar trees rattle. Black Owl felt the presence of the elders. Twenty soldiers of the United States Army were on the ground, looking up in horror and terror, anticipating a very painful death.

Black Owl then asked for his warriors to stand the men up, and tie their arms behind their backs, not too hard, just to keep them from doing something foolish. Some of the soldiers were crying, some had the look of seeing a ghost. There was no resistance or shenanigans of any kind from them. Some of them started to pray, looking up at the sky. The words to the "Lord's Prayer" were heard as if it were a recital.

Black Owl then instructed Swift Eagle, Red Stick, and Broken Talon on what he wanted the warriors to do. The soldiers were lined up in a row. He then spoke to his warriors,

"My brothers, these men are no threat to us or our village. To take their lives in battle would bring dishonor to us and our great people. We would be killing them not in self defense, but in vanity. Vanity is a detour off the Red Road, and we do nothing which takes us away from our ideals as children of the Great Spirit. "

"These men are not worthy soldiers, their horses are weak and sick. They were sent here to antagonize us into attacking them, and killing all of them. Then, the United States Army could declare us ruthless savages and get permission to storm across the Crooked Fork and try and kill us, and our women, elders, and children. Watch."

Black Owl went over and took a revolver out of one of the soldier's holster. Once again, he opened it and showed everyone the bullets that were in it. He then put it to his own head, much to the shock of everyone watching, and pulled the trigger six times. Again, the warriors heard six clicks.

"These men were sent here with guns that do not fire and horses that may not get them back home. They do not have any idea why they are here. If war is to be fought at all, it is to be done in honor. There is no honor in making battle with these men."

"I pray every day that I can learn to understand and respect my white brothers, but when this is the way they treat their elders, I cannot do that."

Black Owl then pulled his knife out of its sheath and walked to the first soldier in line. The man started wailing like a baby. More immediately followed, sensing death was near.

"My brothers, follow me. To touch an enemy brings more honor than killing him. The enemy knows he could have been killed easily, but his life was spared. He knows that he was owned. There are twenty men here for you to count coup on. Many many warriors have died not counting that many coups in their lifetime. Do not harm these men in any way, they are terrified now, and more so to come. Look into their eyes, and you will see the anguish of fear and hopelessness. It is never pretty. We let these men live, praying that one day our brotherhood will be recognized and honored by them too."

Black Owl then took the flat side of his knife, and rubbed it sideways on the man's shoulder. He continued down the row, followed by his warriors. Some of the soldiers passed out from fright, but the counting of coup went on.

The horses of the soldiers were then brought to them, and Black Owl personally untied each man. He then spoke in English,

"Soldiers, you are free to return to where you came from. You broke a treaty by coming to this side of the Crooked Fork. We will escort you to the river, so you can go back where you belong. I have many warriors here who would love to kill a bluecoat, for the pain the bluecoats have brought our people. Each one of them has touched you. Should you come over here again, you know what you will be up against, and you may not find us in this benevolent mood."

The soldiers mounted their horses, and headed east to the river, about 25 yards in front of Black Owl. As they approached the Crooked Fork, a long gauntlet was set up. Lame Bear's warriors were on the south side, and Running Elk's on the north. Black Owl rode ahead, and guided the soldiers to ride through the gauntlet. The soldiers again started crying out of fear. Each warrior they passed by reached out a coup stick, and touched the soldiers. When they rode completely through the gauntlet and into the river, the men kicked their horses to make them run as fast as they could. The three war parties watched them until they were out of sight. It felt wonderful to be a warrior on this day.

"Do not grieve, misfortunes happen to the wisest and best of men. Death will come, always out of season. It is the command of the Great Spirit, and all nations and people must obey.
What is past and what cannot be prevented should not be grieved for misfortunes do not flourish particularly in our lives, they flourish everywhere."

Big Elk

**This book as well as other books
and artwork by Dan Barden
can be purchased online
with all major credit cards at:**

www.hawkesong.com
website of Hawkesong Press

Dealer Inquiries may be made to:

sales@hawkesong.com